I0673876

HER WEREWOLF CHAMPION

JODI VAUGHN

NEWSLETTER SIGNUP!

Copyright © 2015 by Jodi Vaughn Previously titled Darkside Of the Moon

All rights reserved.

No part of this book may be reproduced in any form or by any electronic or mechanical means, including information storage and retrieval systems, without written permission from the author, except for the use of brief quotations in a book review.

❀ Created with Vellum

ACKNOWLEDGMENTS

I want to thank the very talented artist AndE Allison for allowing me to write her into my story and for creating and donating art inspired by DARKSIDE OF THE MOON to Authors After Dark.

This book is dedicated to anyone who's been haunted and defined by their past. You are good enough. You are strong enough. Most importantly, you have the power to create a beautiful future because you deserve it.

CHAPTER 1

*L*ittle Rock, Arkansas

Zane Steele rubbed his aching thigh as he waited in the hallway for admittance into his Pack Master's office. Despite being Barrett Middleton's second-in-command over the Arkansas werewolves, Zane still had to wait like every other fucker when he was summoned.

Life of being an Arkansas Guardian.

Guardians were the elite werewolves who protected the Pack and civilian Weres from discovery. Although the military knew about werewolves, and used them in the armed forces, the rest of the human population had no idea they even existed.

It was better for everyone this way.

"What's up, man?" Jaxon, his fellow Guardian, ambled down the hall from the direction of the gym as sweat dripped off his massive body and onto the concrete floor. He was shirtless, and his black gym shorts hung low on his hips, revealing a wall of muscle.

The Guardian Quarters housed not only the Pack Master's office but also the Guardian barracks and a state-of-the-art gym where the alphas could release some steam in between missions.

"I'm here to see Barrett." He narrowed his eyes at Jaxon and wondered why he hadn't scented the Were before he'd seen him. His leg wound must be distracting him more than he liked to admit.

"When you're done, come out to the gym. I need someone I can spar with that I won't hurt." Jaxon grinned over his shoulder as Lucien approached them.

"Whatever, fucker. I totally had your ass." Lucien shot Jaxon the bird before giving Zane a "what's up" nod.

"If we fought, I'd break you in two, Jaxon." Zane gave his Pack brother a rare grin.

"Well, we can't all be as bad-ass as you. Some of us have to be charming and damn good-looking." Jaxon smirked and his blue eyes flashed.

"Yeah, that's where I come in." Lucien shoved Jaxon hard into the wall. Jaxon stumbled but quickly regained his balance and snarled.

"Easy, children. I don't have time to break up a fight before my meeting." Zane disparaged them as his hand brushed his sore thigh. "Always the enforcer." Jaxon's gaze dipped to Zane's thigh.

He stopped rubbing his wound when he realized Jaxon was staring at him.

"Is your leg not healed yet?" Jaxon frowned.

"Just taking its sweet-ass time. That's all." Zane shrugged, crossed his arms over his massive chest, and tried to ignore the pain.

A Guardian should be in control of himself at all times.

Even in control of his pain. He was one of the highest-ranking Guardians in Arkansas, and he wasn't about to let a leg injury inflicted from some meth head turn him into a pussy.

A few days ago, Zane had taken Lucien and Jaxon on a recon mission to investigate a werewolf who was suspected of making crystal meth. A dilapidated house in rural Arkansas had been the base for the drug operation. Barrett had given Zane the green light to take down the suspect and destroy the drugs before they could be circulated in the werewolf population.

They'd busted into the old house and soon realized that the suspect was not alone. There'd been fifteen wolves crammed into the tiny house, and judging from their stench, they were all red wolves. The wolves had drawn on them and, without backup, the Guardians were forced to fight for their lives.

They'd managed to take out and kill eight of the wolves immediately upon entry. Five Weres made it out the door, but Jaxon and Lucien had quickly caught up to them. They'd shifted and fought, eventually killing all five Weres.

Zane had stayed in the house with the other two wolves. The Weres, sensing they couldn't take him in their human form, both shifted and attacked him. He'd fought them off in his human form before deciding to shift to give himself a better advantage. Right before he shifted, one of the wolves had shoved him backwards into the table where they'd been cooking meth. The cylinder that held the drug had shattered, and a shard of glass had gone into his thigh.

The pain only pissed him off further.

He'd dug the glass out of his thigh, then looked up as he gave them a slow, evil grin. Anger pulsed through his body. One werewolf shot out the door and escaped. Zane launched himself at the other werewolf before he could follow suit. He shoved the shard from his thigh into the drug dealer's neck. Blood spurted out like a fountain. The scent fueled his rage, and he proceeded to rip the red wolf's throat out.

That was weeks ago. As a werewolf, he should have healed by now, but his injury was still bothering him. He couldn't shake the feeling that something was off.

Barrett's door swung open, and the imposing leader stepped out of his office.

The Guardians all stood a bit straighter as their Pack Master, Barrett Middleton, stood in the doorway. Well over six foot five inches, Barrett looked a bit like the Viking god Thor, with his shoulder-length blonde hair and intense eyes.

"What the hell is this? A tampon convention? Don't you all have something to do?" Barrett glared at Jaxon and Lucien.

"Yes, sir." Jaxon fought a grin before he and Lucien strode off in the direction of the barracks, leaving Zane standing alone.

"Zane, come on in." Barrett stepped aside and motioned with a nod to enter.

Zane made his way to the chair in front of Barrett's massive desk. His gaze flitted to the Arkansas Guardian shield that hung on the wall before meeting Barrett's gaze.

He waited for his Leader to speak. A mission. That's exactly what he needed. Being on a mission always made him feel his best. He needed this to get his mind off his thigh and focus on what was important. His work. He needed something where he could shut down some miscreant werewolves and get to feeling normal. To feel in control.

"I need you to do something for me." Barrett eased his large, muscled body into the chair behind his desk and slid a brown file over to Zane.

"A mission?" Zane frowned as he picked up the file. He wondered why he hadn't heard anything through the grapevine about any upcoming trouble in Arkansas. Usually he had some idea of what was about to go down before it did. He didn't like to be left out of the loop.

"Not exactly." Barrett rubbed his hand across his face and met Zane's gaze. "I've got to host the Pack Master meeting here in

Little Rock. I've got the Pack Masters of Tennessee, Mississippi,

Alabama, and Louisiana coming in, and I can't leave." "Sounds like a recipe for a good time." Zane snorted.

"Sounds more like a dick-measuring contest," Barrett deadpanned.

"Well, boss, if that's the case, then you don't have any competition." Zane laughed.

"Damn right I don't." Barrett reached his arms up and rested them behind his head.

"So what is it you need me to do?" Zane leaned forward with interest. Politics of the Packs always interested him. As a high ranking Guardian, he had ambitions to one day be Pack Master himself.

"I've got some new recruits who need their Guardian ink."

Zane curled his hands into fists and struggled to keep his expression neutral. His heart rate sped up.

"You're talking about Braxton and Jayden." He forced the words out of his mouth.

"Yeah." Barrett lifted his chin. "You got a problem with that?" "No problem," he lied. He had a big fucking problem. Not with Braxton. He liked the tattooed-up werewolf with the blue hair. Braxton had a protective streak a continent wide when it came to women, and Zane could respect that.

"Come on, Zane. I've known you for years. I may be your Pack Master, but I know you better than anyone else in the Guardians. I know you even better than those two

5

lunkheads, Jaxon and Lucien." Barrett glared at him with laser focus. "Do you have a problem with your assignment?"

"Like I said, there's no problem." His history with Jayden was nobody's business. Zane was loyal to Barrett to a fault, but when it came to his family, that was a whole other animal. Where Zane had grown up with an intact family that had rules and structure, Jayden had been raised by his granny, who didn't exactly follow the rules. He'd realized from his brief interaction with the old lady that she didn't have a filter, and didn't know the meaning of discipline.

"Perfect." Barrett eased back into the chair, resting his elbows on the leather armrests, and steepled his fingers. His blond hair brushed his shoulders as he cocked his head and studied Zane.

"The appointment has already been made. Since we've got two Guardians and each tatt is time-consuming, it's going to take a while. So you'll need to leave tonight for Jonesboro."

"Anyone else going?" Zane remembered getting his Guardian tattoo. The tattoo of wings that spanned his back, with eyes that peered out symbolized you belonged to the Guardians, the elite werewolf soldiers. Being a Guardian was a high honor that involved sacrificing yourself for your Pack and maintaining control of yourself at all times.

It rankled him that Jayden was about to get his ink. Control was not a word he would ever deem fit for Jayden.

"You can take Lucien." Barrett shrugged. "I need Jaxon to go check out a situation in the southern part of the state."

"Sounds good." He stood, and his thigh screamed in protest. He forced his expression to remain neutral under the ache. He had hoped a weekend of rest would facilitate the healing, but that wasn't happening.

Maybe a hard ride on his Harley was just the thing to work the soreness out of his thigh and the anger out of his soul.

CHAPTER 2

Skylar Wade stood in the middle of the metal shed and forced back the angry tears threatening to fall. She'd erected the shed in the backyard of the house she was currently remodeling so she'd have a safe place to lock up her tools at the end of each workday.

She fingered the lock that had been cut away with bolt cutters and swallowed a growl. She'd had the shed delivered and set up when she started working on the house to keep drug addicts from stealing her tools at night. There'd been a recent string of robberies at construction sites, so she'd taken precautions. Or so she'd thought. In the end, even the lock hadn't deterred the thieves. They were like rats determined to get into a refrigerator filled with cheese.

"Assholes." She slammed the door of the shed. The metal clanged loudly, along with the beat of her heart echoing in her ears.

She was on deadline to get this house finished, and now, because some of her tools were gone, she was going to fall behind.

She was counting on the money from this job so she

could place a bid on the old abandoned apartment building on the south side of town. Her vision of remodeling the apartments as a home for runaway girls who needed a safe place had been her mission in life.

Having grown up neglected, where she'd been raised by an abusive father, Skylar wanted to give girls a different life. She wanted to give them a different childhood.

In giving back, maybe she could set her ghosts to rest, and finally have some peace.

She pulled out her cell phone and pulled up her list of workers. She needed to let them know that there was going to be a late start to the work day. No need to tell them about the break-in. It would only worry them, and they might start looking for work somewhere else.

She glanced at the time on her phone. She had just enough time to replace her tools before the workers got there.

And this time, she was adding a heavy chain and lock to her list of supplies.

CHAPTER 3

"*I* packed some cookies." Granny, in her orange and pink muumuu, ambled over to the group of bikers and proceeded to hand out brown paper sacks to each of the Guardians.

Zane frowned but didn't make eye contact. He figured it was best not to encourage the old woman.

"Granny, it's not a picnic." Jayden grimaced as his grandmother handed him a bag and patted his cheek.

"But these are your favorites. Snickerdoodles." Granny pursed her lips together.

"Thanks, Granny." Jayden smiled and unrolled the top of the bag to peer inside.

Zane clenched his teeth. Just being around the ass-kisser, Jayden, made him want to pummel him in the face.

If they didn't leave soon, he was going to do just that.

Granny stopped in front of him and held out a bag. He grunted but didn't take the bag.

"Come on, son. You need to keep up your energy." Granny smiled.

"Thanks, but I'm good," Zane insisted. He was acquainted

with Jayden's sex-toy-selling granny. What the hell did she think this was? Going off to day camp?

There was no love lost between him and Jayden Parker. Zane had caught the Were with his sister, Katy, doing the nasty. He'd come over to check on Katy only to find Jayden buck-ass naked and in her bed. Before he could get his hands on the asshole, Jayden had jumped out the window. Without his clothes.

"Are you diabetic? Gluten intolerant? Have an allergy?" Granny cocked her head and tapped a finger to her lips as she tried to diagnose him.

Braxton and Lucien snorted behind him. He turned and shot them the bird over his shoulder before turning his attention back to the elderly woman.

"I'm not diabetic, gluten intolerant, or allergic. I just don't want any," he snarled.

"Granny, give them to me," Jayden called out after he straddled his Harley Davidson Breakout. He smiled as Granny passed him a second bag.

Zane slid onto his red Breakout and tried to think of anything other than kicking Jayden's smug ass.

"When are you coming home?" Granny asked.

"I don't know. Hopefully in a couple of days. Check on Haley for me, will ya?" Jayden said.

"Of course. We've got a lot to do to get ready for this wedding." Granny waggled her gray eyebrows. "I know just what kind of present to give you for the honeymoon. I got a new shipment of edible…"

"Enough," Zane called out. He didn't need whatever was about to pass through the old lady's lips to stick in his head for the duration of the trip. "Let's ride."

He started his engine and the bike rumbled to life. The street came alive with the roar of Harleys.

Zane looked at Lucien before pulling out and down the

street. He glanced in his rearview mirror as the other two Harleys peeled out and followed behind him in formation.

He loved his Harley like he loved his brothers. Except for one.

He narrowed his eyes on the newest member to their group.

Jayden.

He'd never had a problem with another Guardian before.

Not until Jayden.

It was causing him to seriously rethink the qualifications for being a Guardian. Something he would have to take up with

Barrett.

*Z*ane lowered his speed as they entered the city limits of Jonesboro, Arkansas. His headlight cast a streak of white against the black asphalt. The sun had long since dropped behind the horizon, cooling things off to a manageable temperature, despite it being July in the South.

The city had grown since the last time he'd been here, and he was surprised at how spread out it was quickly becoming. They would definitely need to place Guardians in this area soon.

He turned onto Main Street and drove to the end of the street before making a left. He ignored the people on the sidewalk who stopped to gawk at the group of bikers entering their town.

They probably thought they were up to no good.

Too bad they didn't know the truth. Guardians were the only thing keeping the human population safe from rogue werewolves who wouldn't think twice about killing for shits and giggles.

Zane slowed his speed as the Moon Goddess Tattoo Shop came into view. He pulled into the parking space in front of the shop. The rest followed suit and parked behind him. He put the kickstand down and dismounted his Harley.

Lucien peeled off his fingerless motorcycle gloves and shoved them in the pocket of his leather jacket. The Were rolled his leather- and steel-stud-clad shoulders as he cast his gaze across his surroundings. His jet-black hair was wind-blown, and he didn't bother smoothing it out. His piercing green gaze was hidden behind sunglasses that he really didn't need, but that didn't impede his keen eyesight. Lucien had taken to wearing his Oakleys all the time after he'd met Damon Trahan, who never took his off.

"Afraid you're gonna get a callus?" Zane snorted. He and Jaxon constantly rode their fellow Guardian about wearing gloves. Lucien had no qualms about dressing the part of a biker. And judging from the looks the humans on the side-walk were shooting their way, the humans believed the whole gang to be dangerous.

They weren't wrong.

The owner of the Moon Goddess Tattoo Shop, Matt Townsend, ambled out of the shop. He had sleeve tattoos on both arms and tattoos circling his neck. Zane bet the guy had his entire body tattooed, but he couldn't confirm what hid underneath the jeans and T-shirt.

"Zane, good to see you, bro." Matt was the official tattoo artist for the Guardians in Arkansas. The job of marking the specialized soldiers had been handed down to him from his father, who had inherited it from his own father. The artist was always a civilian werewolf, and they were well compensated.

Every state had its own tattoo artist. Before they had started tattooing the backs of Guardians, they had used other ways to mark their soldiers. Less pleasant ways, like branding the flesh.

Nowadays, it was all about the ink.

"Hello, Matt." Zane gripped Matt's shoulder in a half hug as he slapped the civilian Were on the back. "I see you were waiting for us."

"Actually, I was about to take a smoke break." Matt grinned sheepishly.

"Disgusting habit. You need to give it up." Lucien smirked as he greeted the tattoo artist with a hug.

"You're right, Lucien. But I need a little excitement in my life. I don't get to go around shooting shit up and ripping out throats like you guys do." Matt chuckled as he lit up.

A thin wisp of gray smoke trailed up to the inky sky and was quickly eaten up by the darkness. Matt inhaled again before he blew out a stream of gray and nodded at Jayden and Braxton.

"They the new brothers?"

"So it would seem," Zane muttered. If he had any say in the matter, he would have voted Jayden's ass out the minute the fucker walked across the Arkansas state line. But it wasn't up to him. It was up to Barrett who became a Guardian and who got cut. That was the one thing Zane couldn't stand—not having a voice when it came to choosing his brothers. If he was going to lay down his life for someone, it better fucking well be someone he gave two shits about.

And Zane didn't give a shit about Jayden.

Matt stuck out his hand and Braxton shook it. "I'm Braxton

Devereaux. Nice to meet you."

"Matt Townsend. I hear you are up in the Eureka Springs area.

I'd love to take my old lady up there for a weekend."

"You should. My mate, Kate, runs a kickass bed and breakfast called the Bella Luna. You want to get your woman all hot and bothered, then that's the place to be." Braxton grinned.

"Sounds perfect." Matt smiled back. "I'll check it out online tonight. Thanks for the info."

Matt turned his attention to Jayden.

"Jayden. Nice to meet you, Matt." Jayden shook Matt's hand. "I appreciate you getting us in this late. I know you'd rather be spending tonight with your mate."

Irritation flared in Zane's stomach like a stick of dynamite. Why the fuck was Jayden rolling in and acting like he was the one in charge?

"What he would rather be doing is working instead of listening to you wasting his time," Zane snarled.

Jayden straightened and turned to face Zane. "Just saying hello. Didn't know I was wasting his time."

"You know, that's the thing about you, Jayden. It's always about you and what you want." Zane curled his fingers into fists as anger boiled into every recess of his cells. His heartrate jumped into overdrive as his breathing quickly turned into a heated pant. Everything in his body screamed for him to shift.

"Look, man, I suggest you turn down your arrogance a notch or two. I do not like what you're giving me." Jayden bowed up and took a step toward him.

Rage filtered through every cell of his body as bloodlust sucked him under like an ocean wave. The only thing he wanted was to rip Jayden's throat out.

"Dude, your eyes," Lucien warned.

Zane didn't need the warning. He already knew his eyes were turning yellow, signaling his impending shift into wolf.

"Dial it back, Zane." Lucien placed his hand on Zane's shoulder.

Zane stiffened for a brief second before knocking Lucien's hand off.

"Don't fucking touch me," he growled. He sucked in shallow breaths as his heart drummed in his chest, ready to explode.

"Look, man, what's your fucking problem? You've had an issue with me ever since I joined the Guardians." Jayden narrowed his eyes and took another step closer. "You're all about the Guardians being brothers, but you sure as shit aren't living it."

Rage exploded within Zane as he lunged for Jayden. He caught the Were around the neck with one hand and knocked him to the ground. Jayden swung and hit him in the face. The taste of blood filled his mouth, feeding his anger. The sound of ripping clothes turned to white noise in his ears, but Zane couldn't stop what was coming next. He knew he was shifting, right there in front of God and everyone. He couldn't stop it.

"Fuck." Lucien put all his massive body weight behind the shove that sent him and Zane tumbling into the dark alley between the tattoo shop and a consignment shop. They landed with a thud on the concrete. The jolt rattled Zane's teeth.

"What the fuck is going on?" Lucien demanded near Zane's ear. Zane had shifted and was now in wolf form while Lucien sat on top of him. "You can't fucking shift in public, bro. If Barrett finds out, he can have you kicked out of the Guardians. Or worse."

Zane struggled to get his urge to maim and kill under control. He caught a glimpse of Jayden walking into the alley, and he let out a warning growl.

"What's going on?" Jayden asked.

"Just stay back," Lucien warned. "Go inside with Matt and get started on the tattoo. We'll be in a minute."

Jayden nodded before disappearing inside with Matt.

When Zane heard the door close, he twisted his body in

one fluid movement and bucked Lucien off. He leapt to his feet and snarled at the Guardian.

Lucien glanced down at his leather jacket. "Fuck. You made me scuff up my jacket, dick." He glared at Zane. "What the fuck is wrong with you? You know you can't be shifting in public like that. And why the fuck aren't you shifting back?"

Zane lifted his head to Lucien. Rage filled his veins, and the urge to rip Lucien's throat out swamped him like an ocean wave.

What the fuck was wrong with him?

Why couldn't he shift?

And why the fuck did he want to hurt Lucien?

Zane sprang to his feet and stared at Lucien through wolf eyes. He nodded in the direction of the shop, hoping his friend would get the hint and leave.

"Something's been going on with you for a while." Lucien cocked his head. "You know, you've not been yourself since we

went on that last mission. Did something happen?"

Holy fuck.

The drug takedown.

Getting stabbed in the thigh.

The wound not healing.

Lucien was right. Ever since that night, Zane had been on edge, ready to fight. He'd tried to cover it the best he could by pushing his body to the limit during workouts and training exercises, but even after that, he craved the taste of blood.

Barrett would kill him if it turned out that it was impossible for him to shift back. Or worse, kick him out of the Guardians.

He'd rather face death than lose his job. His job was his purpose, his life.

He gritted his teeth and nodded toward the door.

"Fine, man. I get it. You don't want to talk about it." Lucien held out his hands. "I'll go keep an eye on those two while you pull it together. I'll bring you some clothes when I come back." Lucien stormed down the alley back to the entrance of the tattoo shop. Zane kept his gaze trained on him until Lucien disappeared from view.

CHAPTER 5

*S*kylar had managed to play off the late start to the
workday as the sheetrock not being dropped off on
time. Thank god the guys believed her. Her guys were hard
workers, and she didn't want to lose them to another
contractor.

They'd managed to put in half a day's worth of work
under the grueling Arkansas sun before they began to lose
daylight.

She looked around at her ragtag construction crew, and a
smile grew on her lips. They might not look like much, but
they were the closest thing she had to a family.

"Miss Skylar, what are your plans for tonight?" Tony gave
her a shy smile. The sweat on his olive skin gave off an
iridescent sheen. The young man had just moved to Jonesboro from Mexico to live with extended family. His goal was
to earn enough money to one day go to college.

"I think I have date." She arched her brow as she dusted
off her jeans.

His smile slipped and he glanced down at the ground.

She inhaled a sharp breath, realizing he'd mistaken her words.

"I have a date with a bubble bath and a beer," she assured him.

Tony brightened and he quickened his pace as he began loading the tools back into the shed.

"He's got a crush, Skylar." Hector elbowed her in the ribs.

"Hector, he's just a kid."

"He's only a few years younger than you. Plus, he's legal." Hector's bushy brows shot up. "In age and immigration."

It didn't matter what his age was, she wasn't interested in dating. She had too much stuff on her plate as it was. A guy would just add to her to-do list.

She'd been lucky to land this contracting job. She'd not met the owner of the house in person—she'd put her bid in online, and follow-up communication had been via phone or email, since the owner lived out of town. She wondered if the reason she was picked for the job was because the owner was a female and had been willing to give her a shot. It didn't matter—she needed this job. She was going to make a nice profit once it was finished, and unlike past jobs, the owner didn't bother her much.

Apparently, the owner lived in Little Rock with her husband and wanted to fix up her house so she could sell it. With the new hospital that had just been built, housing prices in Jonesboro were skyrocketing.

She remembered first looking at the old farmhouse set on the outskirts of town. There had been some kind of explosion that had destroyed part of the building. The kitchen and the back had suffered the most damage. Fixing it up was an undertaking for sure. The house was probably fifty years old, and the electrical and plumbing had to be redone to bring it up to current code before remodeling could begin. Now, two months into her project and on schedule, it was starting to take shape.

Her heart leapt in her chest as she thought about her next project.

The apartment building. Once this job was finished and she had her tidy profit, she was going to move on to what she really wanted to do. Make a difference for girls in trouble.

She'd often wondered if her life would have turned out any different if she'd had a safe place to stay, instead of being forced to survive in the hell her father had raised her in. As a child, she'd suffered enough from neglect, dirty clothes, not enough food, and no heat in the trailer in winter. But once she'd entered puberty, things had gotten worse. Her father had turned a blind eye when his perverted friends had taken an interest in her. Her only moments of escape were the times she spent at her friend Katy's house. But even then, she couldn't completely escape hell. Those dark nights in Katy's parents' home, she'd lain awake worrying about dawn. She knew once the sun came up, she was going to have to leave her safe haven and go back to the hell known as her father's trailer.

If she could save just one girl, then her life wouldn't be a total waste. She jumped when her phone buzzed in her jeans pocket. Pulling it out, she headed over to her truck to have a little privacy away from her construction crew.

"Hello?"

Her heart slid into her stomach as the voice of the owner of the house began telling her that she was moving up the deadline for the finished remodel. Her mind raced as her mouth went dry. How could she have this finished in time? She was pushing her workers as it was. Not to mention the break-in. If her tools were stolen one more time, then there would be no way she'd make the deadline for finishing the house.

"I see." She tried to swallow around the lump that had developed in her throat. She opened her mouth to tell the owner that she couldn't make that deadline—that it was impossible—but the words froze in her throat.

The conversation ended, and she stood there with the phone pressed against her sweaty face.

CHAPTER 6

*Z*ane's heart pounded in his chest as he concentrated on shifting back to human form.

Nothing.

This wasn't good. Not at all.

If he couldn't control his shift, he was shit outta luck.

He padded down to the end of the empty alley. A chain-link fence was the only thing between him and the street. Remembering the drive into town, he knew that after passing through the neighborhood, it was only a mile or so before a flat field of rice appeared. It didn't provide much cover for a wolf his size, but it would be away from the human population. Maybe he could find an old building to take cover in until he could shift back.

He glanced over his shoulder. He couldn't wait on Lucien to bring him clothes. If Lucien came out and saw that he still hadn't shifted back into human form, then he'd know something was badly wrong. And it would be Lucien's duty to inform Barrett.

Fuck the clothes.

Zane backed up a few feet and took off at a dead run. He

leapt into the air and cleared the top of the fence. He landed on his feet on the cool concrete on the other side. He crouched, listening for footsteps.

Nothing.

Shoving off, he ran for the cover of a copse of trees between two houses. Traffic was minimal. The only people out and about were those coming home from a late day at the office.

His ears perked up as the sounds of voices and laugher and the sizzle from meat being cooked on an outdoor grill drifted around him.

After making sure the coast was clear, he sprinted for the next house. He repeated this, making sure to stay within the protection of the shadows.

Headlights of an approaching car had him ducking behind some shrubbery in front of a window.

"Mommy! There's a monster outside my window!" A tiny child's voice reached Zane's ears.

Shit.

He raced for the next house and took cover behind a large prickly bush to see if anyone would come outside to investigate the child's claims.

As soon as he was out of danger from discovery, he sprinted for the next house.

His heart raced as he spied the isolated, industrial part of town a short distance from the last house in the neighborhood. If he could make it down there without being noticed, just on the other side lay the flat rice fields that stretched on forever.

Seeing his chance, he sprinted toward freedom. His lungs ached as he pushed his animal body, running harder and faster than ever before.

His paws bounded across the hard pavement with each swift step. By the time he reached the first row of rice fields, his heart was about to beat out of his chest. Crouching among the green stalks, he peered around, looking and listening for any signs of a presence, human or animal.

Nothing.

His eyes quickly adjusted to the darkness. He slowly stood, lifted his face to the wind, and inhaled deeply. He caught a faint scent of crops and dirt. Odd. Usually, he would be overwhelmed by the scents of the night. But not tonight.

He listened carefully. Other than the occasional field mouse he could hear scurrying among the rows, he was completely alone.

He needed to find shelter soon before he shifted again.

It was one thing to see a large wolf, but a naked man would stir up more news coverage than Bigfoot, if someone saw him.

Especially in a city as small as Jonesboro.

He sprinted across the rows, heading as far away from the city as he could. He caught a glimpse of a small building off in the distance.

He changed direction and raced for the target. As he drew near, he discovered that the building was a shed of some kind off to the side of a house. He padded over to the abandoned house and sniffed.

He smelled nothing.

He walked up the narrow steps. The front porch had just been added, as evidenced by new boards under his feet. The windows were boarded up, and the front door was locked.

He walked down the steps and headed around the back of the house.

There was a tiny back porch that seemed dated. This wasn't a newly built house. It was a remodel.

He walked up the back steps and tried to nose his way in the back door.

Locked.

Giving up, he headed toward the shed.

The door had a heavy chain around the handles to prevent anyone from entering. Whoever had done that was probably worried about someone stealing their lawnmower.

His heart picked up speed as his thigh ached like fire racing across his flesh.

Picking up the chain between his teeth, he tugged hard.

The chain snapped.

Nosing open the door, Zane headed inside the safety of the shed. Once inside, he pulled the door closed with his teeth. It wasn't locked, but he could probably hear someone if they approached, and would have time to escape before being discovered.

Standing on trembling legs, he looked around at the power tools littering the small building. He nudged some tools aside with his head so he could at least have a space to lie down to recover.

Walking around in a circle, he lay down and curled his body into a ball. Pain raced through his body, replacing the urge to fight.

Whatever had caused him to shift was now trying to make him shift back into human form. And if it he couldn't control it, then he was fucked.

*S*kylar arrived early at her construction site. She knew her crew wouldn't be here for another couple of hours. She'd had a bad dream and hadn't been able to get back to sleep, so she'd decided to start her day early. Her gaze narrowed on the shed and the broken chain that was currently lying on the ground like discarded trash.

"Son of a bitch." She slammed the truck into park and killed the engine. She grabbed her 9 mm out of the glove compartment before sliding out of the truck.

"Druggy asshole better not have stolen my tools." She stomped toward the shed as she clutched the gun in both hands. She was sick and tired of this.

She raised the handgun and aimed it as she reached for the door. She doubted very seriously that the thief was still inside. He would be long gone by now, along with her expensive tools.

But Skylar knew she should never assume anything. She'd learned that much growing up among thieves and drug dealers.

She grabbed the door handle and pulled. The door swung

open and bright morning sunlight washed the interior of the small shed.

Tools hung along the wall, and the table saw was where she'd left it. Everything seemed to be where she'd left it.

Her heart jumped in her throat as she spotted a large, naked man curled up in the corner. He was lying on his side, giving her a view of his muscular back. A large, menacing black tattoo of razor-sharp wings with a pair of eyes peering out spanned his entire back.

"Shit." She gripped the gun in both hands. So the crackhead had gotten high and passed out before he could steal anything. Now it was up to her to handle him.

She reached for her cell phone in her jeans pocket as the naked man began to stir.

"Don't even think about moving, asshole." She glanced down at her phone and managed to punch in a nine. "The cops are going to take your naked ass to jail."

Too bad, 'cause he had a nice ass.

The man tensed and then leapt to his feet in one swift movement. He turned and faced her.

Her mouth dropped open.

He wasn't your typical drug user. No, this guy wasn't skinny, far from it. He was broad, with muscles that spanned his broad chest and six-pack abs. His muscular thighs tensed and moved with each breath, and she felt the hair on her neck stand at attention.

Her gaze dropped lower.

He was huge.

Everywhere.

Her face heated as she dragged her gaze up from his nice package to his face. She shook her head as she tried to focus on his features, in case he made a break for it and she had to identify him to the cops.

His dark hair was short and neat and framed his stunning face. He glared at her with light blue eyes that seemed oddly familiar, and she didn't think she'd ever seen a more handsome yet dangerous-looking man. He probably made women fall at his feet for one minute alone with him, despite the fact he looked more than ready to end your life.

She lifted her face and inhaled as his familiar scent drifted to her.

"You're not human." She cocked her head as she kept her gun trained on him.

Surprise flickered through his eyes, followed by confusion.

"What did you say?" He frowned at her as his nostrils flared.

"You heard me, wolf." She ended the phone call before it went through and shoved her phone into her pocket.

"How do you know that?" He glanced around as his fingers curled into fists at his side. His gaze darted from her to the door, as if he was contemplating whether he could make it past her before she got off a shot.

"I know because I'm a wolf too."

The color drained from his face as he met her gaze. His breathing increased and he looked at the floor.

He shook his head and murmured, "That's impossible."

"Why? Because you don't think I'm pretty enough to be a wolf?" She gritted her teeth. She'd spent her life growing up being criticized because of her red hair and her stick-thin figure. It wasn't until she'd hit puberty and gotten her curves that the men who hung around her dad had started looking at her differently. Being a female wolf was nothing but a curse.

Those old insecurities rose up in her head as she stared back at the dangerous wolf. He had her heart tripping in her chest at how attractive he was. But his dismissive words had turned her blood cold and brought up a past that she'd hidden away.

"That's not it."

"Then what is it?" Her eyes narrowed. She wanted nothing more than for him to hit the road.

He met her gaze. Fear crossed his expression, and her heart tugged in her chest. His eyes widened as he took a step closer. "If you're a wolf, then why can't I smell you?"

CHAPTER 8

*Z*ane stared at the beautiful woman in front of him. Something about her was vaguely familiar. If what she was saying was true and she was in fact a wolf, then he was beyond fucked.

"What did you say?" She frowned as she lowered the gun she'd aimed at him since she'd burst through the door.

"I can't smell your scent." He gritted his teeth until his jaw ached. He glanced down at the injury on his thigh. In addition to losing control of his shift, now he'd lost his sense of smell.

Basically, he was blind.

"That doesn't make sense." She eyed him warily. "All wolves can smell other wolves."

"Yeah, well, apparently my sniffer is on the fucking blink." Along with other things. The floodgates of anger spilled into his veins like a slow-rising river ready to flood the valley.

"How'd you do that?" She eyed him.

"Do what?" He slammed his eyes shut and tried to control his anger. The overwhelming urge to shift was bearing down on him, and he knew if he didn't get her out of here, he might hurt the pretty little wolf.

"How'd you break your nose?" She cocked her head and crossed her arms over her full breasts.

His eyes popped open. She was making fun of him.

A laugh rolled out of him before he could stop it.

"If I knew, then I would know how to fix it, wouldn't I?"

"So how did you end up in my shed?" She glanced around the room, taking inventory.

"I didn't steal anything, if that's what you're worried about."

Her gaze landed between his legs, and her face turned a pretty shade of red.

"Although I wouldn't hesitate stealing some clothes right now." He shot her a grin as she lifted her gaze to his.

"So you shifted without having an extra set of clothes. That's not very . . . smart." She looked up to the ceiling.

"I was kind of in a tough spot."

"Oh yeah? Like you got some bad drugs or something? That kind of tight spot?"

It was obvious from the look she was shooting him that she didn't trust him.

Smart girl.

"I don't do drugs." Drugs did him. Or whatever the hell that was in his system that was trying to fuck him up.

"So why are you in my shed?" Her eyes darted down to his erection and then back up.

He contemplated how much to tell her. So he went for the half-truth.

"I was infiltrating a drug deal by some rogue wolves. Shit went south. I shifted and went after the dealer. Suspect got away, and I was caught without access to my clothes. I saw your building and thought I could hide out until I figured out how to get some more clothes."

"So the tattoo on your back . . . "

"It means I'm a Guardian." He finished the sentence for her.

"I've never met one before. I figured you guys were a myth." She gave him a suspicious look.

"We are only around when there's trouble. I doubt you had any kind of trouble when you were growing up." He snorted and looked around for an old rag or something to at least cover his dick with.

"Right." She narrowed her gaze. "Or maybe Guardians wouldn't even come to the places I grew up in."

He jerked his head back to her and studied her face.

Her straight red hair hung past her shoulders, and he wondered if she smelled like strawberries. She had bright blue eyes the color of a summer sky, and perfect pink lips. Despite the growing heat of the day, she wore jeans that hugged her curves and a sleeveless white shirt that showed off the muscles in her arms. She had an old baseball cap pulled down on her head, and from the looks of the paint stains on her clothes, she was the one who'd been doing work on the house.

And even though he couldn't smell her scent, he was inexplicably drawn to her.

He took a step closer, expecting her to step back.

She held her ground and his gaze.

"How about you go see if you can fetch me up some clothes." He stared down into her face. Fuck if he couldn't get lost in those eyes of hers.

She smiled and placed her palm in the middle of his naked chest. His dick ached and swelled from the innocent touch.

"How about you fetch them up yourself. I'm nobody's bitch." She turned on her heel and marched out into the yard.

Zane watched her disappear into the house and scratched his chest. Usually women would do anything he asked.

Not her. No, this female was different.

He glanced down at his erection and groaned.

Not only was he fucked, things looked like he wasn't going to get fucked either.

CHAPTER 9

"*W*here the hell is Zane?" Barrett growled.

Lucien grimaced and held the phone away from his ear. He hated lying, and he avoided it at all costs, especially when it came to Barrett. He knew his Pack Master could make his life a living hell if he so chose. He also knew Zane, and what had happened last night wasn't like his fellow Guardian.

"He's still at the tattoo shop." Lucien flinched at the lie. Well, Zane's Harley was still at the tattoo shop. That much was true. As far as where the fuck Zane had gone after Lucien had gone inside last night, he didn't have a fucking clue.

"How did the tatts go? Anyone cry like a bitch?" Barrett asked.

"Not that they would ever admit. But I think Jayden got glassy eyed once or twice when they were working across his spine." "Yeah, that always smarts a little," Barrett said.

Lucien relaxed a little. As long as Barrett didn't ask about Zane again...

"Tell Zane to answer his fucking phone. I need to talk to

him." "Will do, boss." Lucien ended the call and shoved the cell phone back into the pocket of his leather jacket. He glanced around the street before entering the alley by the shop.

Why would Zane leave without telling him where he was going? And why the hell would he leave when he had no clothes to change into?

He frowned as the faint coppery scent of blood drew his attention to the ground. He crouched and ran his hand across the dark spot on the concrete.

"Zane's blood." He'd noticed the blood around Zane's mouth after Jayden had punched him. He stared at the smear of red on his fingers before swiping them across a patch of green grass that had stubbornly pushed through a crack in the concrete.

The question was what was going on in Zane's head. He'd never seen the Were get so heated so quick before.

He knew there was some history between Zane and Jayden when it came to Zane's sister, Katy, but from what he could tell, that shit had happened years ago. Jayden was mated, and was even getting married to Haley.

There had to be something else going on with his partner.

He pulled out his phone and glanced around, making sure he was alone. He'd left Jayden and Braxton inside to get their tatts. When they'd asked about Zane, he'd covered and said that Zane had been called away for some mission from Barrett.

He punched in some numbers on his cell and waited for the call to connect.

"Jaxon, we've got a problem."

CHAPTER 10

Skylar stormed into the house, putting some much-needed distance between herself and that gorgeous werewolf who had her body overheating like an air conditioner in the middle of an Arkansas summer.

He hadn't recognized her. After all these years, he hadn't recognized her, yet she hadn't forgotten him. Story of her life.

The arrogant asshole had another think coming if he thought she was going to do his bidding. Her father had tried to control her, and she wasn't going to let another man, or wolf, try to do the same.

She stomped through the house and set the gun down on the board that was lying across what would soon be the kitchen island.

The smell of wood shavings and paint had always calmed her down before. Maybe it was the possibility of creating something new and starting over.

Right now, the scent wasn't working.

What the hell was Zane doing here anyway? It unnerved her that a Guardian was poking around her construction site. She didn't need him around bringing up her past. She was in a different place in her life now. She was productive and happy and meeting her goals. Bringing up stuff from the past was only going to hinder her future.

She fished her cell out of her back pocket and pulled up the phone option. Her finger hovered over the number pad as she contemplated her choices.

If she called the cops, then he would probably make trouble for her, since he was one of the well-connected Guardians of Arkansas.

She could call the Pack Master of Arkansas and lodge a complaint about finding one of his Guardians naked. She seriously doubted he would even listen to her, and she certainly didn't want to make trouble with the Pack. She didn't need that. She just wanted to be left alone to build her business and make the town a good place to live.

She sighed and shook her head.

"I guess it's up to me to handle him." The thought made her stomach churn. She pulled out her phone and dialed Hector. She quickly told him to call her workers and tell them they were getting a late start on the day again due to materials not being delivered.

Maybe if she was lucky, she could find Zane some clothes and he'd leave.

Skylar had never been lucky in her life, so maybe it was time for her luck to change.

*Z*ane found a drop cloth with paint stains crumpled up under some buckets in the corner of the shed. After shaking it out, he wrapped the material around his waist and headed after her. He didn't need that woman calling the cops—or worse, his Pack Master.

He needed to find that drug dealer who had been in the meth house that night. He needed to know what exactly he'd been infected with so he could find a cure.

He hurried across the yard as the early morning sun peeked over the horizon. It wasn't even full daylight and the air was already stifling. It was going to be another hot July day.

He walked around to the back door and noticed the door was ajar. He made it up the steps and into the kitchen and froze.

"What are you doing?" He kept his voice low as he studied the cell phone in her hand.

"Well, I was going to call the cops to get you off my property. But I figured if I could find you some clothes, then maybe you would leave on your own." She lifted her chin.

"Clothes would get you one step closer to getting rid of me."

"Promise?" Her sapphire-blue eyes narrowed. It was clear she didn't believe a word he was saying.

"I swear it."

"Fine. Stay here while I run to the consignment shop."

"Consignment shop?" He hadn't intended for her to buy him clothes. He'd figured she could borrow them from a friend or relative.

"Yeah. Consignment shop." She propped her hands on her hips and scowled. "Look, I know you Guardians are used to wearing high-end jeans with all that money you make, but I can't afford designer jeans." She turned on her heel and headed for the door. She stopped at the door and shot him a glare over her shoulder, holding up her finger in warning. "And don't touch anything while I'm gone."

He stood in stony silence after she slammed the door behind her.

Never in his life had anyone talked to him that way. Especially a female.

Well, there was this one female, but that had been a very long time ago, and she had been just a child and full of spunk. That child had the same flaming red hair and startling sapphire blue eyes as this woman—

His breathing hitched as déjà vu settled over him.

He might have lost his sense of smell, but his sixth sense was screaming at him that this was the same person.

After all these years, he'd found that little girl, and now she was all grown up.

Skylar plunked down some bills as the old man at the cash register bagged up her purchase. She'd managed to find some jeans and a T-shirt that would fit the werewolf. She'd even found some secondhand boots that she hoped would fit. She'd not really looked too hard at his feet when he had been standing in front of her naked. But if the size of his boot correlated to the size of his package, then the large boots would fit.

"Thanks." She snagged the bag off the counter and headed out the door. She walked past the tattoo shop and glanced down at her phone to check the time. She'd wasted enough hours today taking care of some Guardian werewolf who probably wouldn't even lift a finger to help her if she needed it.

Distracted by her cell phone, she slammed into a wall of muscle. She stumbled back and caught her balance before she fell.

"Sorry." She glanced up and gave the stranger an apologetic smile. She froze, her blood turning to ice in her veins.

"Skylar Wade. Long time no see." The large Were grinned

as his vulgar gaze roamed up and down the length of her body.

"Hershel." She clutched her phone in her hand like a weapon and forced herself not to look away. Hershel Baker had been one of her father's loser friends. He was always hanging around when she was growing up. Every time she saw him, he was either drunk or high. He'd always given her the creeps, and she'd learned to keep her distance from the Were.

"I didn't know you were back in Arkansas. I thought you were still living in Louisiana." His grin stretched wider, revealing yellowed teeth in a pockmarked face.

"Just here on business." It was a total and complete lie. She'd moved to Louisiana to get away from her father and his nasty drug trade. It wasn't until after he'd died in a drug deal gone wrong that she'd moved back home. She hadn't even bothered going to the funeral. When she'd heard about his death, she'd been relieved. It was one less drug dealer in the world.

She didn't want to be reminded of any ties to her past. She wanted to concentrate on her future. That was why she was back in Jonesboro.

She'd taken her skill for building stuff and her love of drawing and developed her own construction company. She'd built a few houses from the ground up, and had done quite well. "You're looking good, Skylar." He leaned in close and sniffed. "Not a little girl anymore, I see." His lips curved up over his tobacco-stained teeth.

"I see you haven't changed one bit." She took a step back and wrinkled her nose at his scent. Male red wolves carried a musky scent that turned her stomach. Her breathing increased as panic began to settle in her chest.

"It's been too long. We need to get together, get reacquainted." His grin grew to a menacing promise of evil.

"No, we don't." She stuck her hand in her jeans pocket and gripped her keys. She regretted leaving her gun in the truck, but she hadn't expected trouble at the consignment store in the middle of the day.

Hershel's grin faded as his gaze zeroed in on the large boots sticking out of her plastic bag.

"You mated?" He narrowed his eyes on her.

"Yes, I am." The lie came easily enough, and for a brief second, she wondered what it would be like to be bound forever to a werewolf like Zane. What would life be like being cared for and protected by a Guardian?

The whole thing of being protected and loved was such a foreign concept to her. Her own mother had died giving birth to Skylar, and she knew her father had always resented her for it. Maybe that was why he'd neglected her when she was growing up. Maybe that was why he'd turned to drugs, to smother the pain of living without a mate. It really didn't matter. In the end, she couldn't make excuses any more for someone else's choice.

"Who's the lucky guy?" Hershel looked around nervously, as if he expected her mate to appear out of nowhere and demand to know what the hell he was doing talking to her.

A smile grew on her lips as she imagined Zane smashing his fist into Hershel's face right here in public.

"Nobody you know. I met him in Louisiana."

Hershel held her gaze as silence stretched between them.

"I guess he must not be doing too well if you're having to buy clothes from the secondhand store." Hershel whipped out his wallet and tugged out several hundred-dollar bills and waved them under her nose. "I've got more to offer a female than he does. You should really think about that, Skylar." He shoved the money in the wallet and put it back in his jeans pocket.

"No thanks," she muttered to herself. She'd walk bare-ass naked down Main Street before taking one dime from him.

Clearing her throat, she straightened her shoulders. "I've got to go. He's waiting to have lunch with me." She moved past him as she clutched the bag of clothes to her chest. She didn't have to turn around to know that he was watching her walk away. She could feel the heat of his eyes on her.

It made her stomach turn.

When she reached the safety of her truck, she slid inside and locked the doors. She looked around, searching to see if he was still there. She didn't want him following her back to the house. Not that it would matter much. He would probably hightail it out of there once he laid eyes on Zane.

She scanned the sidewalk where they had been standing, but it was empty. He was nowhere in sight.

She noted the time as she cranked the truck. Might as well pick up something for him to eat before driving back out of town.

Maybe after she got Zane dressed and fed, he would leave. Then she could get back to her normal life.

CHAPTER 13

*Z*ane paced the house wearing the drop cloth like a kilt as energy continued to surge through his body.

Since Skylar had left, he'd shifted into wolf twice, and he wasn't sure why.

He couldn't determine what was causing him to shift, or why he couldn't control it. He was trapped inside a body he could not control.

He was fucking helpless, like a damn infant.

He slammed his fist down on the board of the kitchen island.

The wood split in half and slid onto the floor.

The slam of the back door had him turning and bowing up.

"What the hell did you do?" Skylar's expression was full-on pissed off as she pointed to the wood on the floor.

"I got a little jumpy." He flexed his hands as he sucked in a breath.

"Well, why don't you try calming the hell down. I just

started on this kitchen and if you don't stop tearing stuff up, I'm never going to get finished. And when I don't finish, I don't get paid." She shoved the plastic bag into his chest. "I'm not made of money like you. I actually have to work hard for what money I earn."

"Look, princess, I don't know what crawled up your ass, but you need to stop with the attitude. I'm not exactly feeling in control today, so you need to be careful with what you say," he growled.

She spun around on her heel and shot him a glare so heated it should have fried his ass right there in the kitchen.

"Don't ever call me 'princess.'" She shoved her finger in his face. "Let's not forget that it's you trespassing on my project. I have a feeling that the owner of this house would take an issue to having a werewolf hiding out in the shed like a common criminal."

He arched a brow. The pounding of energy in his veins relented a bit. He should be angrier, but instead her tirade amused him. He grinned.

"Skylar, I guess some things never change. You're the same spitfire I remember from when you were a kid." He'd known something was familiar about the female when he'd laid eyes on her.

"So you do remember me." She dropped her hand and stared up at him with her mouth open.

"You are hard to forget," he admitted.

"I was an annoying kid who used to get under your skin."

"You and Katy both did. It was like having two sisters, except one didn't always stay at the house."

"How is Katy?" She swallowed and looked away. "I haven't heard from her since I moved to Jonesboro."

"I wouldn't know." The anger was back in his blood and building to a slow frenzy. He tried to shove away the emotions that only his sister could arouse in him, but it wasn't working.

He'd not talked to her in forever.

And it was all Jayden's fault.

"I've left messages and tried to find her on the Internet, but I can't find out anything. It's like she doesn't want me to find her." Skylar's soft voice had him jerking her head in his direction.

"It's not just you. She's cut her family out of her life," Zane stated. The words settled in his stomach like a sickness. They'd been so close growing up, and now they were strangers.

"Maybe she just needs time to spread her wings. You know, get out from under her big brother's shadow." She chortled. "You have to admit, Zane, you were a bit over-bearing when she was growing up."

"I was not," he thundered. She flinched at the tone, and he immediately wished he could take it back. Instead, he changed the subject. "So you do remember me after all. Why didn't you say something earlier?"

She shrugged her slim shoulders. Her red hair slid like silk across her shoulders with the motion. He inhaled deeply, hoping he could catch her scent, but once again, he couldn't smell a thing.

He felt blind.

"I didn't figure you would recognize me. The last time you saw me, I was a little girl." She walked over to the kitchen window and peered out.

"You've certainly changed. No longer that annoying little girl."

She cast a glance over her shoulder and smirked. "Now I'm an annoying woman."

A laugh escaped his lips.

"Try on the clothes and see if they fit."

He gathered the bag and stepped into the next room to dress.

"Are you expecting your crew to come in?" He tugged on the jeans and was relieved when they fit. She'd guessed his size correctly.

"Yes. And we need to get you out before they show up. I can't do this whole job on my own."

He slid the T-shirt over his head and froze. "You do construction work too?"

She spun around and leaned back against the area where the sink would eventually go. "What's wrong? Don't think I'm capable? I can do anything a man can do, and usually better. It just takes me longer because I like to do it right." Her blue eyes flashed.

"That I can believe."

"What's that supposed to mean?" She uncrossed her arms and frowned.

"When you and Katy were kids and you would come over, you were always straightening up her room because you said it was too messy. You even redressed her dolls because you said their clothes didn't match." He chuckled. It felt good to remember something good from the past instead of feeling the pain of how their family was in ruins now.

She grinned. "I can't help it. Must be my OCD."

"My mom always laughed about it."

He couldn't help but think it had more to do with the environment she'd been raised in.

It was common knowledge that Dale Wade would never get the Father of the Year award. He was a mean old man who'd lost his mate when Skylar was born. The first time Zane had laid eyes on Skylar had been when his sister had brought her over to play. He remembered how dirty Skylar had looked. Face unwashed, dirt under her nails, and dressed in clothes that had not been washed in forever.

She had been no more than four years old, and had been left alone to play out in front of her daddy's beat-up old trailer. His sister had spotted her when her mother had driven by on their way to the grocery store. Katy had started crying and pitching a fit until his mom had pulled over and turned around. His mom had left a note on the door and let Skylar come home to play for the afternoon.

His mother, Victoria Steele, being the kindest woman he'd ever known, had been itching to get Skylar in a tub full of soap and scrub her until she was clean. But she didn't want to embarrass her. So instead she turned on the sprinklers in the front yard and put down a plastic sheet and loaded it down with liquid soap. After she gave her one of Katy's swimsuits she encouraged them to slide. Every time one of them slid down the plastic, they would be covered with bubbles. In the meantime, she'd washed her clothes and dried them so she would have something clean to wear home.

After that day, every time he saw Skylar, she was clean. He didn't know if she was bathing herself or if his mother had a hand in it.

"How's your mom?" Her face softened at the mention of his mother.

"She'd doing well. Still got my dad wrapped around her finger. They just moved down to the coast. She said she was tired of Arkansas getting so much snow. She figured there's a lot less chance of that happening there." He grinned.

"Your parents were always good to me. I didn't know they had moved. Katy didn't say much about them whenever I asked." She smiled. "Richard probably loves the coast. He was always such a big fisherman."

"True." He glanced down at the waistband of her jeans

and nodded at her gun. "I don't think you need that around me, do you?"

"I always carry this when I go to one of my job sites." Her expression hardened. "It seems like I'm always finding drug dealers breaking in at night, to either steal my stuff or to get high."

He froze. "You're not going out at night by yourself to check this out, are you?"

She shrugged. "Sometimes. I already had two thousand dollars' worth of tools stolen. I can't afford to take another hit like that, so I try to ride out to my work sites at night to make sure everything is okay. I don't do it every night, though."

"You didn't last night," he stated. If she had come out to the work site last night with a gun, he would have ended up with a bullet in his hide.

"No, I didn't. And imagine my surprise when I get here and see my shed had been broken into. I was expecting all my tools to be gone. Instead I get a blast from the past who happens to be a Guardian." She cocked her head. Something about him being a Guardian bothered her a great deal. "How did that happen anyway? I figured you would have followed in your dad's footsteps and gone to law school and then made partner at his firm."

Zane shrugged. "Not my thing." He didn't bother telling her that he'd gone to college and actually graduated from law school. He never got around to taking the bar. He had known from the start that law was his father's dream and not his. He'd spent many sleepless nights worrying about disappointing him. So when he'd finally told him, he'd been surprised by his reaction. His father hadn't been disappointed, and he'd told Zane that all he'd ever wanted was for him to find what made him happy and to pursue that.

Being a Guardian was Zane's calling. When Barrett

Middleton had offered him the job, he'd taken the opportunity and had never looked back.

Now that opportunity might be taken from him if he didn't figure out what the hell was wrong with him.

He frowned as he studied Skylar.

"So there are a lot of drugs in town? Do you know what kind of drugs they're doing? Cocaine, heroin?"

"Crystal meth. It's skyrocketed over the last few weeks." She shook her head. "And it's werewolves who are selling it to humans. I overheard a couple of Weres trying to sell it to one of my Hispanic construction workers. Thankfully, he declined. I try to make sure everyone I hire is clean."

She looked at him. "It's weird. Usually drug dealers are users too. But not these Weres. They don't mind selling it, but they sure

as hell aren't touching the stuff themselves."

Zane's blood ran cold. "How do you know?"

"After my worker declined their sale, I walked over to them and took the drug out of the asshole's hand. I opened the bag it was in and started dumping it out on the ground. The guy jumped back, like he didn't want the stuff getting on him. It was weird."

He grabbed her arms and glared down at her. "Did he say why he didn't want to touch it? Did he say what was in it? Did he say what they had added to it?"

"Let go of me." She shook off his hold and stepped out of his reach. His pulse jackhammered in his head as anger once again began to flood his cells.

"He didn't say anything. Just acted weird." She cocked her head. "Zane, why are you so interested in this?"

"It's my job as a Guardian." He squeezed his eyes shut, trying to control his sudden rage.

"No."

"What?" He jerked his head up at her.

"The way you're acting is making me think otherwise. This seems very personal to you." She narrowed her eyes and took another step away from him. Her hand rested on the butt of her gun. "You're not on this stuff, are you?"

"What?" His eyes widened as his heart sped up. Adrenaline pumped through his body at an alarming rate, signaling his impending shift. He turned away from her and grabbed the counter, trying to hold the shift at bay. "Skylar, you need to leave."

"Zane, what's wrong?" He heard the tremble in her voice and sensed her fear. He knew he wasn't going to be able to control himself once he shifted.

"Skylar, leave. Now," he growled as his body began the transformation. His bones lengthened and his tendons stretched to accommodate his wolf body. Fur sprouted across his flesh until he was covered in a furry pelt.

He glanced down at the floor through his wolf eyes.

Fuck.

He'd ruined his clothes. Again.

"Why did you shift?" She spun around to the back door and peered out the window. "Is there danger?" She glanced at him over her shoulder.

Anger and agitation flooded his body at an alarming rate. He glared at Skylar and wanted nothing more than to attack.

What the hell was wrong with him? Why did he want to attack Skylar? She'd done nothing wrong.

"Zane?"

His eyes popped open at the soft sound of her voice.

Her beautiful eyes were wide with concern. The sound of her breathing increased, and his pupils dilated. His gaze drifted down her curvy form as agitation quickly turned to lust.

Run!

He wanted to scream to warn her away from him, but he couldn't speak.

He glanced down, holding himself back from launching at her and tackling her. He could see the scene in his head. Damn, he wanted her. Bad.

Lifting his head to the ceiling, he let out a howl as he lost his battle with his own body.

CHAPTER 14

Skylar reached for the gun as Zane's howl echoed in the house. In wolf form, he had to be at least twice the size he was in human form. Every powerful muscle in his body twitched as if he were holding himself back from something.

His body trembled as his eyes popped open and he narrowed his gaze on her.

Gone was the boy she'd grown up with.

A killer's eyes stared back at her instead.

She aimed the weapon at the large wolf. Her gut clenched as her finger trembled against the trigger.

Did she have it in her to put a bullet in her best friend's brother?

"Zane, I know you're in there." She swallowed the lump that had formed in the back of her throat. "I'm not sure what's going on, but you need to shift back."

His muscles tensed for a brief second. He turned to his left and then walked back to his right. She watched him for several seconds as he paced in the small kitchen.

"It's broad daylight. Someone might drop by and see you.

You know it's against the rules for humans to see us." She gritted her teeth and lowered the gun. If he were going to attack, he would have done so by now.

She frowned as she watched him. "Zane, what's going on?"

He continued to pace the small room, his large body bumping into the corner of the lower kitchen cabinets.

"Shift back so we can talk about this."

He stopped for a second and then glanced down at the floor.

He lifted his head and met her gaze. He made his way to the corner of the room and paced around in a circle before lying down and curling up into a ball.

Her heart sunk in her chest as reality settled over her in a sickening wave.

"You can't shift back, can you?"

CHAPTER 15

Zane stared up at Skylar as he tried to control the rush of adrenaline flooding his veins. Maybe if he could just relax enough, he could shift back.

If he couldn't get this under control, then he was gonna be screwed.

"Zane?" She stepped forward and cast a worried look at him.

He lifted his head and sniffed the air. He still couldn't smell her scent. His gut sunk like a rock.

"Look, I've got my crew showing up soon, so we need to get you out of here." She squatted beside him and cocked her head.

"One of them is a werewolf, and if he sees you in wolf form, he will contact the Pack Master. And you don't want that, do you?"

Shifting in broad daylight was against the code. It was punishable by death because it put the entire species at risk. There was a standing reward for turning in any werewolf who broke the rule. He bet his ass that he'd get turned in for the money.

Skylar glanced at her phone and then back at him. "I can take you back to my place and let you stay there. But we need to leave now before anyone arrives."

He looked up at her, wondering how he, of all people, had managed to get his ass into this position. He had no other option but to do what she said.

It wasn't ideal, but he knew what would happen if he stayed.

She stood and glanced out the window.

He had a bad feeling that her house wasn't exactly isolated out in the country. He definitely didn't need to be in town. The chance of exposure was too great. But right now he was out of options.

"I live in an apartment." She gave him a grimace of a smile.

Things had gone from bad to fucked up in zero point eight seconds.

CHAPTER 16

*S*kylar had barely managed to get Zane loaded up into the bed of her truck before her crew started rolling up to the house in their trucks. She'd covered him up with an old painting tarp. When one of her crew started ambling toward the truck, she'd made up some excuse about having to go check on another property, and had driven away in a rush.

She glanced in her rearview mirror to make sure the tarp was staying tied down. When she saw it held, she breathed out a sigh of relief. She turned off the small country road and onto the main highway.

Sweat beaded at her temple and rolled down her cheek as the summer heat bore down on the metal truck. She sooo needed to get the air fixed. It was going to be one of the first things she did if she ever started making a decent profit from her business. She leaned her head out the window to catch a breeze and caught her reflection in the mirror.

Her red hair had started to frizz around her face, and her cheeks were flushed from the heat. She hadn't bothered with makeup today, and it showed. She didn't normally wear makeup to a job site. If she had anticipated meeting a hot-looking werewolf, then she would have at least slapped on some lip gloss.

She sucked in a deep breath and shook her head.

"I have no idea why I'm even worried about it. It's not like he sees me as anything other than his little sister's friend." She'd always had a crush on Zane when she was little, but as soon as he'd left home to go to college, she'd not seen him anymore. He'd never see her as a woman. Just a kid. Not to mention their social statuses were worlds apart. He was a gray wolf and she was a red.

When she was little, she didn't realize that not all wolves were like her father. It was after meeting Zane's family that she saw that wolves could be loving and protective. It had given her hope that her father could change and be more loving. But that never happened. Things between the gray wolves and the red wolves turned ugly. The males of the red wolf pack had wanted to start taking over the gray wolf territory. When they met to conspire, it had turned deadly as the red wolves began fighting among themselves for more power and more control. By the time she'd graduated, the majority of the red wolves were dead. Not wanting to be the next casualty, she'd moved to Louisiana and gone to college. The last she'd heard, there were very few, if any, red wolves left in Arkansas. So running into Hershel had certainly been a shocker.

She turned onto the street that led to her apartment. She slowed the truck and glanced in her rearview mirror. If she was hot, she knew Zane had to be cooking under that tarp.

She turned into the parking lot of the Castlewoods Apartments. She'd gotten into the apartments when they were first built two years ago. Right now wasn't a good time for her to be a homeowner, since she was so busy with her contracting work and didn't have time to take care of her own home.

She pulled into the parking lot and grimaced. Her apartment was on the bottom floor, but there were a lot of cars in the parking lot, and she couldn't risk letting Zane out here.

She backed out of the parking spot and drove to the end of the lot. The back of the apartments faced a thick, lush tree line that continued on for a while. There was barely five feet between the buildings and the tree line. The only people she'd seen out there were dog walkers who didn't want to clean up after their dogs. If she could get her truck to the back of the apartments and let Zane out there, there would be less chance someone would spot him.

Pressing her lips together, she cast a quick glace around. She listened carefully. When she was sure she didn't see anyone, she eased her truck around the back of the apartments.

Tree branches scraped across the passenger side of her truck, and she clenched her teeth, wondering how much damage it was doing to her paint job.

Shoving her worries aside, she stopped her truck at the back of her apartment. She opened the door. It nudged the side of the building. She squeezed herself through the small opening and stopped at the back of the truck's bed.

"Stay here until I unlock my door." She kept her voice low as her gaze flitted around the wooded area. The last thing she needed was to catch her neighbors' attention by revealing a big-ass wolf in the back of her truck.

She quickened her steps to her door and stuck her key in the doorknob.

"Skylar, hello, dear." Mrs. Nelson cracked her door open and gave her a toothy grin.

Skylar froze as her heart pounded in her throat.

Mrs. Nelson was her nosy neighbor who didn't mind

getting the other tenants in trouble whenever she thought they were up to no good. She'd called the cops twice last week on the poor girl who lived a few doors down for being a prostitute. Mrs. Nelson claimed the girl had a different guy every week. Turned out the girl was a college student who'd taken a part-time job tutoring students in English.

Last month, Mrs. Nelson had called the cops on old man Grissom, who lived in the next building. She told the cops he was growing drugs in his apartment. Turned out he was growing something, but it was only mushrooms in his closet. Not the kind you get high on, either.

After that, Skylar tried to steer clear of Mrs. Nelson. She didn't need the old woman nosing around in her business or her personal life.

"Hello, Mrs. Nelson." She cut her eyes at the bed of her truck sticking out in plain sight. If Zane moved so much as an inch, the old woman would know something was up. Nothing got past her.

"I had to stop by and get some more tools for the construction site I'm working on." She gave the woman a forced smile and hoped it was enough.

"I didn't know you kept tools in your apartment." The old woman narrowed her beady eyes. "Is that even legal?" Shit.

"Oh, I told the landlord about it and he said it was perfectly fine." She dug her phone out of her back pocket and pulled up a number. "Would you like to check with him?" She spoke calmly and evenly, hoping she sounded more confident than she felt.

Mrs. Nelson relaxed. The lines around her eyes drooped and her shoulders slumped. It was obvious she was disappointed she hadn't caught another criminal act.

"How's Luther doing, Mrs. Nelson? I've not seen him around lately." Skylar smiled brightly. Luther was Mrs. Nelson's grandson whom she used to brag about constantly.

A day didn't go by that the old woman wasn't telling anyone who would listen about another of Luther's accomplishments. Four-point-oh in college, majoring in medicine and volunteering at the food bank. That was Luther in a nutshell. He was on his way to being the brightest and the best.

Until he'd been arrested for a hit-and-run and charged with DUI. He'd gotten drunk at the country club, gotten thrown out, and had run over a homeless man who had been crossing the street. After further investigation, it turned out that Luther didn't have a four-point-oh—he'd failed out of college and had continued to lie to his parents about it. He'd taken the money they'd given him for college and used it on weed, booze, and women. It had also been rumored that golden boy Luther now had gonorrhea and gotten some girl knocked up.

After that, Mrs. Nelson no longer brought up Luther to anyone.

Mrs. Nelson's wrinkled face paled. Her eyes widened slightly, and if the woman had been wearing pearls, Skylar knew she would be clutching them in her sweaty palm.

"I've got to go. I have to check on something in the oven." Mrs. Nelson gave her a tight, polite smile that read *F you* and slammed the door. Skylar waited a few seconds, listening as the woman's footsteps clomped away and a tingle of regret slid around in her stomach. She knew bringing up the woman's grandson was a low blow, but it was the only way to get rid of Mrs. Nelson.

Skylar raced to the back of the truck and pulled up the end of the tarpaulin. She was met with a brief growl and Zane's piercing wolf eyes.

"We've got to hurry," she whispered as she stepped back, allowing him space to jump down from the hot truck bed. His long tongue hung out the side of his mouth as he panted.

She bet he felt like he was roasting in the ridiculous Arkansas heat.

She hurried to her apartment and quickly opened the door. He wasted no time and raced inside. She stepped in behind him.

The cool air hit her in the face, as she locked the door and slid the deadbolt. She couldn't tear her gaze away from him as he padded into the living room. He changed course and headed away from the carpeted room and into the tiled kitchen. He paced back and forth and cut his eyes up at her as if trying to communicate.

"Oh, sorry." She hurried into the kitchen and pulled out her largest mixing bowl. Holding it under the faucet, she filled the bowl with cold water and then sat it on the floor.

He dipped his head and lapped up the water in gulps. She opened the freezer and pulled out some ice cubes and dumped them into the bowl.

"You must have felt like you were baking under that canvas." She wiped away an errant drop of sweat from her brow.

He glanced up at her as if agreeing before dipping his head again to lap up the cool water. A slight rumbling growl came from deep within his massive chest.

She'd seen lots of werewolves, of course. But Zane was more beautiful than she'd ever imagined a male wolf could be.

His lush gray fur had specks of silver, and her hand itched to run her fingers through the thick, silky hair.

He cut his ice-blue eyes up at her in an assessing kind of way.

She looked away, embarrassed that he'd caught her staring at him so openly. He probably thought she was some desperate female. Who could blame her? Men like Zane were few and far between.

"I've got to get back to work. Stay here as long as you need. There's some food in the refrigerator if you get hungry after you shift back." She sat the pile of his clothes that she'd gathered up after he shifted on the kitchen counter. They were ruined—he'd busted out of them like a cat out of a bag —but it was all she had at the moment.

"I'll get some more clothes on my way home after work."

He lifted his head from the water bowl and gave her a nod of understanding.

"I don't have a landline, just my cell phone, so there's no way to get in contact with me if you need anything. I'll try to get home as soon as I can." She walked over to the door. With her hand on the cool steel doorknob, she glanced over her shoulder.

He had followed her out of the kitchen and was standing in the hallway, watching her.

"If for some reason you're not here when I get home, I'm going to assume you got tired of waiting around and had other pressing issues to attend to. Otherwise, I'll see you sometime after six."

CHAPTER 17

"*L*ucien, why do I get the feeling you're lying to me?" Barrett growled through the phone.

"Maybe because you're already distracted and upset about having to host the Pack Master summit." Lucien grimaced as he looked over at Jaxon, who was busy checking out a female passing by with shorts so tiny her ass was hanging out.

Jaxon gave the curvy blonde a panty-dropping grin as she looked at him over her shoulder and giggled. Lucien reached out and slapped him on the back of the head.

"Hey." Jaxon shot his friend a glare and straightened from leaning against the brick building on Main Street. It was the weekend, and in a college town like Jonesboro, people were out and about, buying clothes, having drinks, and heading down to the local pub to catch some sports on TV.

The drone of cars passing down the street had Lucien taking two steps into the nearest alley and away from the noise of the little town.

"How's that going, by the way?" Lucien hoped he could

get his Pack Master distracted by Pack business and move his attention off the question of why Zane hadn't checked in.

"It's a fucking barrel of monkeys. I've got Jack Welbourn from Mississippi saying he needs more Guardians, Charles Price from Tennessee saying they want fewer Guardians, and Edward Boudier from Louisiana still giving me shit about his Assassins." Barrett let out a low rumble, and Lucien knew his leader was not going to give the Louisiana leader any quarter for fucking up.

The Louisiana Assassins had shown up a few months earlier in Arkansas, looking to kill Braxton. But when they'd failed to inform Barrett of their presence in the state, it had almost led to a territorial war between the two states. The Louisiana Assassins were clearly in the wrong, but their Pack Master wasn't one to follow the rules unless it benefited him. So the hard feelings remained.

"And here I thought the Pack Masters' summit was all caviar and mint juleps."

"Not likely." Barrett snorted. "Enough with this runaround bullshit, Lucien. Where's Zane?" Oh, fuck.

"I'm not exactly sure. He did say something about following a lead on those meth heads we busted a few weeks ago. He said not to worry and that he'd contact me in a few days." That wasn't happening, since he was holding Zane's dead phone with his free hand. Apparently Zane hadn't shifted back before taking off, because all his clothes, and his cell phone, had been lying in the alley.

Something was very wrong.

"You and Jaxon stay in Jonesboro until he makes contact. I can't afford to lose any of my Guardians. Especially now."

"What do you mean?" Lucien's gut tightened.

"There's more going on with Louisiana than what I'm being told. My instinct tells me that Edward Boudier is taking his vengeance to a whole other level because of the stink I raised with his Assassins."

"That's not good."

"What's not fucking good is Zane not contacting me. You make sure to tell him I'm going to have his ass when I find him."

"Sure thing, boss." Lucien killed the call and looked over at Jaxon, who was now eyeing him with interest.

"What'd he say? He heard from Zane?" Jaxon crossed his arms over his chest.

"Nope. And I got a feeling when he does, it's not going to be good for our Pack brother."

*Z*ane woke up buck-ass naked in the middle of Skylar's kitchen. The cool tile felt good against his overheated body, and he stayed still for a few minutes, reveling in the sensation.

The shadow of the descending sun crawled across the floor, signaling the impending dusk. He frowned, raised himself up, and looked around for a clock. His gaze landed on the microwave. Six thirty.

He'd been asleep for almost six hours, and he felt like he could sleep for six more.

He'd never been like that. Usually, four hours a night made him feel good and rested, but not now. Now he felt like he'd been run over by a fucking eighteen-wheeler and dragged for one hundred miles.

He forced his feet under him and stood on shaky legs. His thigh throbbed. He glanced down. The injury where he'd been stabbed had changed colors. What had been red was now dark crimson with a gray outline around the ragged edge of the cut.

He ran his finger down the injury and flinched at the sensitive flesh.

What the fuck? How had crystal meth done this to him? He was virtually immortal. It didn't make sense.

He swiped his bundle of clothes off the counter and made his way through the apartment to the bathroom.

The apartment was small, with a kitchen that led to the living room. There was a small island that allowed for eating but clearly no room to put in a table. The kitchen counters were clean with no knickknacks or decorations, and the living room only housed a small white couch and a coffee table. He glanced around the room. The few pictures that hung on the wall were all art posters. She didn't have one personal photo.

It seemed impersonal, like a hotel. Usually, women liked to decorate their homes, putting their personal touches on the space. But Skylar hadn't done that. He couldn't help but wonder if her upbringing had anything to do with it.

He entered the bedroom and stopped in his tracks. Here in her boudoir, she certainly didn't skimp.

The enormous king-sized bed made of wrought iron and dark wood was flanked on either side with marble-topped nightstands. The bed was decorated in shades of white and cream, and it reminded him of silky ice cream on a hot Arkansas night. The only colorful things were a couple of froufrou pink pillows on the bed.

The nightstands were identical, with matching white lamps with tassels hanging off their shades. A few books and a candle decorated one of the nightstands, which he assumed was probably the side she slept on. The other nightstand looked a bit lonely with just its lamp keeping it company.

A matching dresser and chest of drawers rounded out the furniture in the room. Yet there were still no personal photos of any kind anywhere.

What had happened to Skylar to make her seem so alone? Where was the little girl he once knew? What had happened in those few years he'd not kept in contact? And why had his Katy not contacted her?

He cast a longing glance at the bed before turning to the bathroom. The last thing he needed was to get his unwashed ass in her pristine bed and stink it up.

He shoved the cream-and-silver shower curtain back and turned the shower on full force. A shower had always perked him up before. Maybe it would do its magic this time.

He stepped into the shower as the steam began to fog up the mirror like a New England morning. He stood under the spray of the hot water, braced his palms on the tile wall, and bent his head, letting the water fall on his neck in a heated rush. He let out a groan as the heat loosened up the muscles between his shoulders, and the tension he'd carried all day fell to the drain with the cascade of water.

He needed to find out what the hell was wrong with him before Barrett found out.

He needed his job—no, he lived for his job. There was no fucking way he was going to let some meth-head werewolf destroy everything he'd created and worked for.

Zane looked up and growled.

He was going to hunt that fucker down and make him fix it.

And then he was going to rip his throat out.

CHAPTER 19

"So you're telling me Zane never came back, or made contact with you, after he arrived?" Lucien narrowed his gaze on Matt. The tattoo artist shifted his weight and looked a little uncomfortable as Lucien questioned him. Lucien always knew when a wolf was lying, and his gut told him Matt was telling the truth.

"Yeah, man. I was too busy getting your Guardian's tatt going to even notice if he came inside or not. You know I do the Guardian ink in the back room, away from the general public." Matt shook his head and laughed. "The last thing I need is for humans to see that tattoo and demand to get the same thing. It is pretty badass, you know."

"Sure is." Jaxon smiled his easy smile and popped a piece of gum in his mouth as he surveyed the latest addition to the tattoo shop in the form of a beautiful human female in jeans that hugged her curves. She gave him a sexy smirk as she bent over to pick up a piece of paper. She made sure to keep her ass up in the air so he could get a good look.

Jaxon growled his male appreciation.

Lucien slugged him in the shoulder.

"Hey." Jaxon scowled and rubbed his arm.

"Pay attention. You're not here to get laid. You're on duty." Lucien's measured words were emphasized as he spat them out between clenched teeth. It was bad enough that Zane was missing and he'd lied to Barrett about his whereabouts. "I don't have time to babysit you or your dick."

"Fuck off. You'd like babysitting my dick too much for my comfort." Jaxon snorted and returned the punch to the arm.

"Is there something I need to tell Barrett about?" Matt arched his brow as he glanced around nervously. "I mean, I don't want there to be any trouble. He's been a good Pack Master and I don't want to piss him off."

"Fuck, no. We got everything under control. As you know, your duty is to keep the Guardians tatted up. That's it." Lucien scowled at the tattoo artist.

Matt swallowed and let out a sigh. "Yeah. The last thing I want to do is be on Barrett's bad side."

"You have no fucking idea." Lucien turned and made his exit out of the Moon Goddess Tattoo Shop. He hurried to his bike and straddled the massive motorcycle. Jaxon mounted his bike and gave him a look.

"So what is it that we aren't telling Barrett?" Jaxon flipped the kickstand and balanced the bike between his powerful thighs.

Lucien gave him a long look. "That Zane has gone rogue."

"Skylar, why does this canvas smell like wet dog?" Hector grimaced as he positioned the tarpaulin on the floor for tomorrow's painting of the sheetrock. Her worker shook his head and said something in Spanish that was probably a lot of cursing. "Did you adopt a homeless animal?" She grinned.

"Maybe." If Hector only knew he was smelling a werewolf and not a dog.

"Okay, I'll be back tomorrow to get the second coat on." Hector stood up and ran his gaze along the wall, assessing the baseboards lined with blue painter's tape.

"Sounds good." She gathered her tools to take out to the shed. Hector grabbed the heavier tools and headed out the door. She shook her head. "Hector, I can carry my own tools. I don't need your help."

"That's what you always say. You need to learn to accept help when it's given," Hector hollered from the yard. "You're too damn stubborn for your own good."

"So I've been told." She snorted and cradled her tools as she followed after Hector. The sun had dipped behind the horizon, leaving purples and pinks in its wake across the sky. Despite the evening's approach, the humidity stuck to her skin like a plastic Halloween mask that had been worn by a sweaty child. Placing her tools inside the shed, she closed the door and placed the new chain and lock she'd picked up in town around the handle. She'd hidden the evidence of the break-in from her workers. She didn't want them asking any questions, and she didn't want them to worry that a meth-head was breaking in and stealing the equipment. If they started worrying, then they'd start looking for another job site to work.

"Nice job today. I'll see you tomorrow, bright and early." She grinned and strode toward the house.

"I can wait on you." Hector scowled.

She stopped and turned to face the man. He'd been working with her since she started, and she'd learned that he was a dependable, hardworking, family man with six kids all under the age of seven. He worked long hours to give his family the life he never had.

"Hector, go home. I'm fine. You are going to miss Cecily's dance recital." Cecily was Hector's older daughter and had been taking dance lessons for the last six months. She loved it more than life, and told everyone she met that she was going to dance in New York City one day.

A smile broke out across the man's face. "She's wearing that pink fluffy thing you gave her."

"It's called a tutu. And I'm glad she liked it." Skylar had found the tutu in a yard sale in one of the upscale neighborhoods in Jonesboro. She knew Cecily would love it the second she'd laid eyes on it.

"Maria bought her a little crown thing to go with it." He pointed to the top of his head.

"Tiara. It's called a tiara." She shook her head. "You've got six girls, Hector. You need to learn the language of all things female." Hector laughed a little. "That's what you need, Skylar. A little girl all your own. You spoil ours too much."

She felt her smile falter. She'd never have a child because she'd never have a mate. She was damaged goods. She knew her place in this world.

She'd accepted her fate long ago.

"You've got enough girls for me to spoil. I don't need one of my own." She plastered on a fake smile that didn't have any roots in her heart and continued toward the house.

"I'll see you tomorrow, Skylar." Hector hurried to his truck. A few seconds later, there was nothing but a cloud of dust where his old truck had been.

She went room to room, making sure no tools had been left behind. She didn't need even one to go missing. She was operating on bare bones.

Darkness had fallen silently. She'd been too busy locking up to notice the time. Pulling out her phone, she frowned as she realized it was almost eight o'clock.

Unease slithered up the crook of her neck and pressed its weight onto her shoulders. She cut her eyes around the dark house, looking for any signs that someone had snuck in while she wasn't looking.

No, that wasn't it. Whatever had her nerves on alert was coming from outside.

Easing up to the living room window, she scanned the yard. Her pupils widened to accommodate the dark.

Nothing.

Stepping away from the window, she shook her head.

"I'm just being weirded out because of Zane." Ever since he'd shown up, she couldn't stop thinking about what kind of trouble he was in. And why he couldn't control his shift.

If any werewolf found out that Zane was out of control, they wouldn't hesitate to turn him over to the Pack Master of

Arkansas. It didn't matter if Zane carried the Guardian mark or not. Easy money was easy money.

And if the Pack Master found out she'd known about Zane and had hidden him, she'd face punishment as well.

"Maybe he'll be gone when I get home." The thought oddly disturbed her. Despite the danger he was placing her in, she didn't want him to leave. There were so many questions she had.

When had he become a Guardian?

How were his parents?

What was going on with his sister Katy?

Unease slipped into a familiar feeling of sadness as she thought of his sister. Katy had been like her own sister until a few years ago. They'd grown up together and had lived together in Louisiana. Now, they were strangers.

Slamming the door shut and turning the lock, she hurried down the steps and across the yard to her own truck. Getting in, she started the engine and locked the doors. Old habits die hard.

She turned on the road and headed back to town and to whatever surprise awaited her.

CHAPTER 21

*Z*ane paced the cramped space in the bedroom as he continued to peer out the window for Skylar's truck.

Where the hell was she?

It was dark, and she should have been home hours ago.

His skin crawled as his heartbeat jumped into a fast rhythm. His body hummed with energy, and he wanted nothing more than to shift and run off his anxiety.

The lock in the front door clicked, and he stopped in his tracks.

"Zane?" Skylar's soft voice called out from the other room.

Relief and irritation hit him square in the gut like a sucker punch. Fisting his hands, he stormed into the living room.

"Where the hell have you been?" he thundered.

"Working." She pulled what smelled like food containers from brown paper bags and narrowed her eyes at him. "Why are you naked?"

He glanced down at the towel wrapped around his hips and then scowled at her.

"I ruined my clothes, remember?"

"I know, but you could have at least put my robe on instead of that."

"Stop changing the subject. It's been dark for hours. Where have you been?"

"I had to stop and get you more clothes. This time I bought extra." She dropped the bag on the kitchen counter. She jerked her head back at him and shot him a glare. "Wait, do you think I ratted you out to your Pack Master?" Her lips pressed into a white line as her gaze narrowed even further. "I may not be a gray, but I don't ever rat out my race. Ever." She shoved away from the kitchen counter and stormed past him toward the bedroom.

"Skylar." He growled and caught her elbow.

"What?" She spun around and faced him. Anger flashed behind those blue eyes, and something shifted in his chest. His body heated, and his breathing turned to a pant.

He couldn't smell her—hell, he couldn't smell anything. He shouldn't be feeling this. Not at all. He tried to release his hold on her but couldn't as his heart thumped loudly in his chest.

He growled low and deep as he pulled her into his arms. The second her body sunk against his, all he wanted was her.

Her lips parted and her pupils dilated. He knew then that she felt it too.

He slammed his mouth across hers, sealing the taste of her onto his mouth and searing it into his brain. She tasted like cherries, and he wanted more. He wanted so much more.

Lust licked every cell of his body until he was trembling with animalistic need.

She didn't fight him and instead relaxed into his hard embrace. Her hardened nipples pressed into his naked chest through her thin T-shirt. His hand slipped around and up under the back of her shirt to brush her naked skin. Her heated skin grazed his rough palm, and he pressed her closer as he deepened the kiss.

She moaned and then fisted her fingers into his short hair as she sucked his tongue into her sweet mouth.

Fuck, she was going to give him a heart attack before he got inside her.

"Skylar." Her name hung between them like a soft prayer. He was used to bedding women, but none like her. None like Skylar.

"Stop talking and take my clothes off." Her feminine hands reached for his towel and pulled. The terry cloth landed in a puddle on the tile floor of the living room. Good thing he'd closed all the curtains; otherwise, they would be giving the public a show.

She glanced down at his straining erection. Her mouth dropped open and she murmured a feminine sound of appreciation.

"It's my turn." He tugged her T-shirt over her head and tossed it in the air. A lacy white bra was the only thing covering her beautiful breasts.

He unsnapped her jeans and pulled the fly down in a slow and torturous motion. As much as he wanted her, he didn't want to hurt her. Judging by the look on her face, she'd not been with a lot of men. Especially men as well-endowed as he.

He shoved her jeans down to her ankles and knelt in front of her. Lifting one leg, she balanced a hand on his shoulder while he pulled her jeans off. He looked up at her. Her red hair curtained her face, and her full lips were parted as she panted. He gave her a wicked smile.

He hooked his thumbs in her white lace thong and tugged it off. He ran the pad of his thumb along the red landscaped landing strip down to her clit. She shivered and gripped his shoulders with both hands, and he felt her legs tremble under his hands.

His heart beat faster as he nudged her legs farther apart. He kept his gaze fixed on hers as he pressed an open-mouthed kiss to her wet heat between her creamy thighs.

Her taste exploded on his tongue as he licked at her wet flesh. He growled like a bear needing more of the sweet honey that only she could give.

"Zane, don't stop." She gripped his head and pulled him closer as her legs began to tremble.

He grinned with male satisfaction and continued his assault between her thighs. Hell couldn't pull him away from her. He was quickly becoming addicted to her. At the moment, he really didn't give a fuck.

"Oh god," she cried out as her head fell back against the wall. He gripped her thighs, holding her upright as her orgasm swept over her. He didn't stop licking and sucking until she was nothing but a quivering mass in his hands.

When she went limp, he steadied her as he stood up. Cradling the back of her neck, he pulled her in for a kiss.

"I think I almost blacked out," she moaned against his neck.

She was warm and soft and tasted like heaven. For the first time in a long time, he felt like he'd found himself.

CHAPTER 22

*S*till shaking from the force of her orgasm, Skylar pulled back enough to stare up into Zane's dangerous ice-blue eyes.

She'd been around him for her growing-up years and had never seen this passionate side of him before. He was always in control—of his emotions, his expression, his future. Now after going down on her, he looked like he was ready for seconds.

His generous mouth curved upward into a sensual smile that belied the dangerous teeth lying on the other side of his lips. He was a bit deceiving if you didn't know any better. To the casual observer, he looked like any other hot guy.

To the werewolf population, he was a lethal Guardian.

"You taste like sunshine." He growled low and deep, and it made her skin pebble with desire.

"Yeah, well, let's see how you taste," she volleyed back.

His pupils dilated even further until all she could see was black.

Running his hand up her back, he pulled her into his straining erection. With his free hand, he twisted a piece of her hair around his finger, lifted it to his nose, and inhaled. He frowned as if remembering he couldn't scent her.

She ran her fingertips across his furrowed brow.

"Which sense would you rather have? Smell or taste?"

A wicked grin stretched his lips. "If it involves tasting you, definitely taste."

Her heart thumped in her chest at his words, and her stomach warmed. She'd never wanted anyone like she wanted Zane, yet the ghosts of her past were edging their way forward from the corners of her mind like wisps of steam.

Not this again. I will not be a prisoner of what he did. I'm not that little girl anymore.

Zane leaned down; his warm breath tickled her cheek and sent licks of delicious pleasure deep within her stomach. "You're beautiful."

She sucked in a breath to try to calm the vibrational arousal racing through every inch of her body.

"I've been called a lot of things, but beautiful is not one of them." She chortled nervously as she licked her dry lips.

He leaned back, capturing her gaze with a hardened one. "That can't be true."

Her face heated and she shifted her weight. She should never have said anything. He probably thought she was an insecure woman looking for a compliment.

She took a deep breath and grabbed his hand. "I think we started a job that needs finishing." She tugged on his hand as she took a step toward her bedroom.

"Didn't feel like a job to me." He grinned, making her body heat with lust.

She didn't think she'd ever needed a male as much as she needed him right now.

Once they were inside her bedroom, he spun her around in his arms.

"You taste like heaven." He leaned down and covered her mouth with his. His tongue snaked between her parted lips and licked every inch of her mouth like she was dessert.

When he finally pulled away, she couldn't breathe.

"You've certainly changed since I last saw you, Skylar." His gaze roamed down her body like a heated caress.

Those ghosts that had hung back in the shadows of her mind lurched forward. She sucked in a deep breath at his words. Cold reality skittered across her flesh, and she pushed him away and wrapped her arms around herself like a shield.

"I had to grow up pretty fast, Zane. Not everyone was born with a silver spoon in their mouth like you."

"I didn't mean . . ." He narrowed his eyes and reached for her, but she shook her head, not letting him finish.

"It doesn't matter. This was a mistake. We are a mistake." She took a step back from his warmth, determined to be strong.

She didn't need this right now. Getting involved with a man— even just for one hot night would complicate her plans for the future. She needed a clear head, and whenever she was around Zane, he made her head spin

"Are you scared of me?" He cocked his head and shot her a heated gaze.

"Of course not." *I'm scared of letting you see me. Emotional scars aren't that sexy to a male like you, who could have the finest female in the state.*

Though the words were silent, they brought tears to her eyes.

Her heart rate shot up as she grabbed her robe and escaped into the kitchen, putting much-needed distance between them. She'd gotten the apartment because it was safe and the price was right. At the time she hadn't cared that it wasn't that big. But with Zane standing in the middle of the room and taking up space with his huge muscles and sexy vibe, it seemed the size of a shoebox.

Securing her robe, she opened the refrigerator and pulled out two beers. She shoved one at him as she passed him on her way to her bedroom.

What she needed was a shower. A very cold shower to wash his scent off her and clear her mind.

He caught her arm before she made it into the bathroom and spun her around. She knew she needed to get away, but the warmth coming off his hard, naked body was too much of a temptation for her to step away.

He was going to be her kryptonite.

"Skylar, talk to me."

"Zane, I don't..."

Knock, knock, knock.

Zane tensed, and Skylar cut her eyes up at him.

"Skylar, is everything okay in there?" Mrs. Nelson called out from the other side of the door.

Skylar rolled her eyes to the ceiling and let out a sigh. She mouthed "Be quiet" to him as he made his way into the bedroom and closed the door.

Taking a deep breath, she strolled over to the door. Before reaching for the doorknob, she cut a glance over her shoulder to make sure Zane had stayed in the bedroom. The last thing she needed was for Mrs. Nelson to see she had a visitor. That old lady would want to know everything about Zane, from his blood type to his shoe size. Not to mention that if she suspected he was staying with her, that old bat wouldn't hesitate for one second to rat her out to her landlord.

The last thing she needed was another pair of eyes on her.

Gripping the doorknob in her hand, she flung open the door.

"Mrs. Nelson. What can I do for you?" She plastered a

hard smile on her face and met the woman's beady gaze. She cocked her head around Skylar's shoulder, trying to get a look inside.

"I thought I heard noises. I know you don't have a TV, so that couldn't be it." She swung her gaze back to Skylar. It held an intensity she wasn't used to feeling from the frail lady.

"I had the radio on. That's probably what you heard." She forced herself to hold the woman's gaze.

"Didn't sound like a radio to me. Much too loud." Her eyes narrowed into snake-like slits.

"Oh, well, it's my new sound system. It can get pretty loud." She gave her neighbor a sheepish grin. "I'm so sorry to have bothered you with it. I'll make sure I keep it turned down." Skylar eased the door closed, but the woman put her foot in the way, preventing it from shutting.

"Are you okay, Skylar? You're acting a little strange."

"I'm just exhausted. Been busting my ass to get this job finished."

Mrs. Nelson frowned her disapproval at the coarse language.

"Sorry. I meant 'butt.'" Skylar blushed.

"Hmmm. Well, try to keep it down. You don't want to be known as the troublemaking neighbor, do you? Why, just look at how everyone avoids Samantha in 243 after that whole debacle. Good girls are quickly becoming a thing of the past. You don't want to get a bad reputation, do you?" A low rumble came from behind her bedroom door. Skylar forced out a laugh.

"As you can hear, I think my plumbing is acting up again. Better go check on it." She slammed the door in the old woman's face. Leaning back against the door, she let out a sigh.

Her bedroom door eased open and Zane stood there looking pretty pissed off.

She held her fingers up to her lips and turned to take a look out the peephole. Mrs. Nelson closed her door behind her.

Spinning around, she leveled a glare at him. "I told you to be quiet," she hissed.

"And I don't like how that old hag talked to you." He curled his fingers into fists as anger shot from behind his eyes.

"I learned a long time ago to ignore people's opinions of me." She shrugged and headed into the kitchen.

"It's never okay for people to talk shit, Sky."

Her heart tumbled in her chest at his endearment for her. It had been a long time since she'd heard him call her by that nickname.

"Whatever. Look, we have bigger issues at hand." She waved her hand up and down his body. "You apparently have a problem with not being in control of your shift. And I am on an impossible deadline to get the house finished."

She shoved past him into the bathroom. Before she shut the door, she looked at him. "Which is another reason we can't happen. We don't fit into each other's world. We can't ever happen, Zane."

CHAPTER 23

"What the fuck just happened?" Zane murmured.

One second he was a breath away from sinking himself into heaven, and the next she was cold as a snowdrift.

No woman had ever turned him down. Ever.

Stomping into the kitchen, he opened the fridge and pulled out another beer. He frowned as he surveyed her meager shelves which contained only sandwich meat, left-over lasagna, a package of sliced cheese, eggs, bacon, and a six-pack of beer. No wonder she was so thin. The girl needed to eat.

He popped the top of the glass bottle and turned it up. He downed half the beer before he heard the shower turn on in the bathroom.

His dick hardened further as he imagined Skylar stepping into the tub, the water glistening off her perfect, silky skin. She'd probably lean her head back and let the water cascade off her auburn hair and down her slender back. He imagined her arching into the stream as she ran her fingers through her hair.

Lost in his vivid image of her, he leaned back against the kitchen counter and closed his eyes. She would be soaping up the washcloth and then caressing her breasts until they were soapy mounds. She'd run the cloth down across her flat stomach and make little circles before inching down farther until she touched her sensitive flesh between her long legs.

His eyes popped open and he downed the beer. His body was on fire and on edge, and if he didn't do something, he was going to go crazy.

"Fuck it." He slammed the empty beer bottle down on the counter. Reaching for a stack of napkins, he grabbed a handful. Walking into the living room, he planted himself on the couch and leaned back. Taking his hard dick in his hand, he began to stroke, imagining it was her hand around him instead.

If he wasn't going to have Skylar tonight, then he damn sure was going to have the fantasy of her instead.

"*Y*ou needed to see me, Barrett?" Damon Trahan ambled into Barrett's office and gave his Pack Master a nod in greeting. It had been well after midnight when he'd been summoned, and he wasn't feeling too friendly toward his boss.

"I did." Barrett shot him a scowl before turning his attention back to his computer screen.

"Look, I get I'm low man on the totem pole and all, but could you maybe next time wait until morning? You know how Ava hates it when I get pulled out of bed."

"Stop right there." Barrett's fingers froze on the keyboard and he held up a large hand. "Not another word about what I interrupted between you two in bed. That is not an image I need in my head."

Damon's lips tilted up ever so slightly. He liked that Barrett wasn't lusting after his woman. He knew the hard-ass Pack Master saw Ava as a little sister. Good thing, too. He would hate to have to kill his superior for looking at his mate's fine ass.

"Fine. No play-by-play." He leaned back in the chair

facing Barrett. "But you have to admit this is becoming a habit—you getting me out of bed at all hours of the night."

"You're a Guardian. It's part of the job description," Barrett deadpanned as the computer screen drew his attention once again.

"Be honest, man. How many times have you called Jayden out at midnight for a meeting? Or Lucien? Hell, any of the other

Guardians, for that matter?"

"Jayden doesn't go to bed at sundown like you do, jackass."

"I don't go to bed early." Damon frowned and crossed his arms over his chest. "Is that what that fucker said?"

Barrett cracked a smile. "That's what Ava said. She told me she needed you home by six."

"I'll have a talk with her." He loved his mate, but she sometimes pushed the line when it came to the Pack Master.

"Speaking of Ava, how's her remodel coming?"

"Good. I think she wanted it done faster so she can get it on the market while the housing market is hot. She doesn't want to move back to Jonesboro, which makes everything easier on me." Ava's house had been bombed by red wolves as payback after he'd rescued her from captivity. Forced to go on the run with her, he'd quickly realized he'd fallen in love. In the end, he couldn't let her go. After judgment was meted out against the kidnapper, Barrett had mated Damon and Ava together.

"She got someone good, I hope. Contractors will fuck you over if you're not careful. Especially if they are dealing with a woman.

They think they can pull one over on them." Barrett snorted

"Actually, this contractor is female."

"No shit." Barrett nodded in appreciation.

"Yeah. She and Ava seemed to click. Plus, she came in under bid and promised to be on schedule."

"Just wait. I'm sure some unexpected expense will crop up and you'll get it up the ass."

"It's Ava's business. I try to stay out of it. I did tell her it was a bad idea to hire someone she'd never met in person. She's working with the contractor via Skype and phone."

Barrett froze. He turned to give Damon his full attention.

"Well then, I think it's time for Ava to take a trip over to Jonesboro to check on the progress. I mean, it would only make sense to check in."

"I've tried to get Ava to go, but she doesn't want to be without me."

"Which is why you're going with her."

CHAPTER 25

"Fuck." Lucien glanced at his ringing phone and grimaced. Even if he answered it, he wouldn't be able to hear anything over the music in the club. The smoke alone was killing him. After making sure Jayden and Braxton had gotten their tatts, Lucien had sent them on their way back to Little Rock. He and Jaxon had stayed behind to try to find out what was what with Zane.

"What?" Jaxon craned his neck to see the caller ID. "Dude, it's Barrett. You need to answer it."

"No shit." The ringing stopped and Lucien shoved the phone into his back pocket. They'd hoped they could find a lead on Zane at Jonesboro's only nightclub, but so far they'd come up empty. It was like he'd disappeared off the face of the earth.

"So what's the plan?" Jaxon glanced at him before turning his back on yet another human female who'd eased onto the bar stool next to him in the crowded club.

"The plan is to avoid Barrett. Find Zane. And get to the bottom of what the hell is going on with him."

"You don't think he's using, do you?" Concern creased Jaxon's face.

"What?"

"Meth. You don't think he's using meth."

"For fuck's sake. It's Zane we're talking about. He's the most in-control guy I know. He hardly ever drinks." Lucien slammed down the shot of tequila and motioned for the bartender to give him another.

"Yeah, then what the hell is up with him?" Jaxon dragged his eyes away from a passing female with skinny jeans that hugged every curve. He met Lucien's gaze with a worried frown.

"I don't know, man. All I know is he's not been right since the drug takedown. Were you in the house after it was over? Did you see him do anything? Take anything?"

Jaxon shook his head. "I barely left his side for two seconds. Besides, they were still cooking the shit. The product wasn't even ready for distribution." He glanced around, making sure no one else was listening in to their conversation. "Hell, it was still liquid. Or it was until Zane bumped into it, and it destroyed what was left."

"It doesn't make sense. All I know is something is going on with Zane and if we don't find out what it is before Barrett does, he's going to be out of the Guardians." Lucien sucked back the rest of the bitter beer.

"At best."

"What do you mean?" Lucien narrowed his gaze.

"Getting kicked out is going to be the best outcome. I know Barrett, and he's a stickler for upholding the Lupine Law. If Zane doesn't stop shifting in public or if he's on drugs, he's going to be facing a Tribunal. And we both know what that means. He's going to get taken out. Permanently."

"*W*here the hell are you going?" Zane thundered.

Shoving down her anger, she maneuvered around Zane's large body and snatched her keys and backpack off the kitchen counter.

"I need to go check on something." She spun around and faced him, not ready for her body's reaction to seeing him standing there wearing nothing but a sheet wrapped around his lean waist, intensity sparking from his eyes.

After their argument, she'd shown him some sheets and a blanket so he could sleep on the couch while she tossed and turned in her own bed.

He didn't understand what she'd been through—hell, most people wouldn't. But once he found out what she was— damaged—then he'd leave her alone soon enough. A Were of his status demanded a pure female, unblemished and perfect in every way.

She didn't want to ruin him too.

"It's fucking one o'clock in the morning. You're not going anywhere this late." His eyes blazed as he stared her down.

He probably meant to intimidate her and frighten her into submission. What he didn't realize was that it was turning her on instead.

Stupid girly hormones.

She shifted her weight, thankful his sense of smell was on the blink. Otherwise, he'd know how attracted she was to him right now.

"I have a business to run. And that involves checking on my work sites to make sure some meth-head isn't stealing my shit." She stormed toward the door and turned. She waved her hand up and down his body. "And you can't come because you're naked. The last thing I need is to be driving around Jonesboro with a naked man. Or wolf."

It was definitely the last thing she needed. How could she concentrate with his male scent filling up her truck like an aphrodisiac?

"The last thing you need is to take on a thief by yourself. You could get hurt or worse."

Her gaze drifted south to where his fingers clenched the sheet. She swallowed back the lust that was currently warming her stomach and threatening to take control of her senses.

She shook her head. "I've got a gun. I'm not running into danger like you think. I do have a brain, you know."

"Skylar, don't you think about opening that door." His growl sent a delicious shiver across her heated skin.

A smirk played on her lips as she turned the doorknob and flung open the door.

"Don't wait up." She slammed the door behind her just as he let out a growl.

Tightening her grip on her backpack, she hurried to her truck before he could follow.

CHAPTER 27

"*D*amn it." Zane started for the door just as his sheet fell to the floor.

She'd done it. She'd actually disobeyed him and left.

He glanced down at the erection he was sporting and shook his head.

She disobeyed him and it made him hard. Again.

How fucked in the head was that? His body surged to life as the urge to shift took over. His skin prickled and his gut clenched as rage fueled his body. He sucked in a deep breath to control his breathing and force his body to stop the shift.

His gaze landed on the door. Once he shifted, there was no way he was going to be able to open the door and go after Skylar. But if he left now, someone in the apartment complex might see him once he shifted into wolf.

Both fucking choices sucked.

"Fuck it." He opened the door and sprinted for the back of the complex. If he was going to shift, it was better to do it away from the security lights that surrounded the front of the building.

He made it down the back steps and raced to the tree line

just as he heard Skylar's nosy old neighbor call out her name.

The old bat was probably up late doing some TV shopping for some cat figurines or some shit like that.

His body trembled as the shift washed over him. He stayed in the shadows of the trees, hoping the old woman wouldn't walk out her door. If she saw him, she would probably call animal control— or worse, the local news channel— with reports of a bear.

Finally the door shut, and he relaxed. The old woman was smart enough not to come looking out into the dark. Good for her. Never knew what might be lurking in the shadows.

Zane lifted his head at the star-speckled night sky. The balmy Arkansas air did nothing to cool his overheated body.

No wonder so many wolves preferred the cooler climates like Colorado and Montana.

He cut his eyes and surveyed his surroundings. It didn't matter that he couldn't scent Skylar to get a trace on her. And it didn't matter that he'd been covered with a tarp while being transferred here. He didn't need any of that to find his way back to the house that she was working on. When his sense of smell had failed him, his hearing had been amplified. He'd been doing more than just hiding under that tarp while being driven down Arkansas roads. He'd been listening to his surroundings and learning how to get back to where he'd been.

His ears perked up as the shrill of a train whistle cut into the black of the night. His mind quickly retraced the direction toward Skylar's destination.

He sprang off his feet and raced along the tree line out of sight of humans.

His gut told him that something was off where Skylar was concerned.

He didn't know what it was, but he damn well intended to find out.

CHAPTER 28

"*I* want to go too." Granny propped her hands on her skinny hips, making her yellow and green muumuu crinkle up a bit, and frowned.

"Granny, this is not a vacation. It's just a quick trip to go check on the progress of Ava's house." Once they got that house fixed and on the market, he'd feel relieved. It had nothing to do with money. Hell, as a Guardian, he did pretty fucking well. All Guardians did. He just didn't want Ava to have a house or a place she might run off to if she got pissed at him.

Getting rid of the house would be just one more step in healing the feelings of abandonment from his past.

"I didn't say it was. I'm just bored."

"What about running your"—he cringed as he forced the words out—"business?"

"I need a little break from all that selling. Why, the only time people come up to me anymore is to find out what flavor edible underwear I have. I feel used." Granny pursed her lips into a thin white line.

Damon felt nauseated.

"Besides, I need a little time away to refresh. And I want to check out what Jonesboro has to offer. Heard they have a cute little farmers' market on Saturday and a street festival every Thursday night."

"First of all, I'm not going to just hang out. I have things I need to get done. Besides, I'm taking my Harley, and Ava's going too, so there's no room for you."

"We can put the sidecar on it and there will be room for me." Granny's weathered face brightened.

"Oh, hell no. No one is putting that monstrosity on my Harley." Damon fought back a shiver. The Guardians were still giving Jayden hell about when he'd discovered the sidecar on his beloved Harley Davidson Breakout, with Granny in the passenger's seat. It just wasn't a good look.

"What are you guys talking about?" Ava walked into the living room, pushing a rolling suitcase.

"Wait. Hold up. What's with the suitcase? You know there's no room for it in my saddlebags. Just take one set of clothes." He shifted his weight as the estrogen in the room doubled.

"I can't travel with just one change of clothes. What if the weather changes? Or it rains? Or I spill something? Or we find a nice restaurant? Not to mention my shoes. I need my shoes, Damon." Her eyes widened frantically.

"What are y'all discussing?" Jayden strolled in with Haley snuggled under his arm. Jayden planted a kiss on her lips when she gazed up at him.

"Damon won't let me go to Jonesboro with him and Ava." Granny pouted and gave Jayden puppy eyes.

"Damon, stop being a dick and take Granny." Jayden glared at him.

"Jayden, language," Granny quickly corrected.

"Why don't Granny and I take my SUV and you ride your Harley?" Ava said. "That way we can pack whatever. Plus, I've been dying to check out this new Arkansas artist, Ande Allison. I've seen her artwork online, and I want to buy some before she gets expensive."

"Good idea, dear. Get her on the way up." Granny smiled and patted her hand. "I hope she's better than that artist who did that canvas for me in Little Rock. I asked for an abstract garden. I got a picture of a vagina." Damon's stomach clenched as he shook his head, trying to dislodge that mental image.

"Granny, please." Jayden rubbed his eyes.

"That's a good idea. You and Granny ride together and we'll meet up at the house." Damon knew better than to argue with either Granny or Ava. Besides, this way he could do a little investigation on his own without Ava knowing what he was up to.

"I'll pack a picnic." Granny clapped her hands together and grinned.

"It's only a two-hour drive, Granny. And it's hot as hell out there. We're not doing a picnic." Damon looked to Jayden for support, but his fellow Guardian just shrugged his massive shoulders.

"Dude, you're fighting a losing battle. Just go with it." Jayden smirked as he and Haley made their exit.

Damon gritted his teeth. Fucking Jayden.

Zane's body pulsed with adrenaline as he raced across the rice fields toward the city. For a small town, it sure had a lot of nightlife going on. He'd encountered a couple of teenagers parking on a back road and had scared the shit out of the guy when he'd leapt out in front of the car. The guy had screamed and shoved his girlfriend in front of him, which had earned him a well-deserved slap in the face.

Then he almost got hit by a truck when he jumped across the railroad tracks. The asshole must either have been drinking or doing drugs, because he leaned out the window and shot him the bird. The guy didn't seem fazed that he'd just seen a large-ass wolf.

Zane's paws hit the ground in a rapid staccato. His lungs ached as he sucked in breaths with each bounding step. His heart beat between his ears, and his body echoed with the need to find Skylar.

And when he found her, he had half a mind to take her over his knee and...

His body warmed at the thought. Not of hurting her, but

the idea of having her bent over her kitchen counter—or better yet, the bathroom sink—as he sunk his dick into her tight little body.

He shook his head and continued his breakneck journey in the direction he knew she would be headed.

She was too damn stubborn to listen to anything he said. Coming out here this late at night was a bad idea. Even if she was carrying a gun.

The full moon illuminated the white farmhouse sitting up in the distance.

Relief poured off him in waves as he noticed her truck turning into the driveway and coming to a stop. She kept the headlights on as she got out of the truck.

He gave her credit for that move.

He kept his gaze locked on her as he hurried though the rice field. Unease pricked the back of his neck, alerting him to some unseen danger.

A rustle came from the back of the house, followed by a large, dark shadow. Whoever or whatever it was, was quick. Skylar, sensing the danger, lifted her gun in the direction of the noise.

Zane's heart squeezed in his chest. He pushed his body harder, running as fast as his legs could carry him. Ignoring the sting in his lungs, he growled as he rushed to close the distance between him and the danger that threatened Skylar.

The shadow ran straight for Skylar and tackled her to the ground. The sharp echo of a gunshot pierced the quiet darkness.

Zane's gut twisted as his blood ran cold.

Please let Skylar be okay. Please let her be okay.

He broke free of the rice field and ran into the yard. As he got close, he realized the shadow must be some kind of were-wolf due to its size.

Zane leapt through the air and knocked the assailant off

Skylar. They tumbled to the ground in a tangle of limbs. He twisted his body and pinned the attacker to the ground.

The guy was definitely wolf due to his size and the way his eyes were changing colors from blue to yellow, signaling an impending shift.

The werewolf drew back his arm and slammed his fist across Zane's face, catching his nose in a stinging blow and knocking him off. Rage propelled Zane forward, and he launched his body as the guy began his shift into wolf. He didn't have but a moment with the upper hand. Once the guy shifted, they would be evenly matched.

He lunged and caught the guy around the throat. A strangled gurgle slid out from his lips as Zane bit down harder. The guy dropped to the ground.

Bloodlust seeped through his entire body as the assailant's blood trickled into his mouth. He craved the coppery taste. He wanted more.

A whimper from behind had him freezing. Letting go of his hold on the werewolf, he glanced around for Skylar. His gaze landed on her a few feet away. Sprawled on the ground and lying perfectly still, Skylar let out another soft whimper.

He leapt off the attacker and hurried to her side. He lifted his paw to her face and then cringed. He needed his human form. He needed to help her. Why the fuck wasn't he shifting back?

He searched her face, frantic for signs of any injuries. Had she been shot? Was she hurt? And how the hell was he going to be able to help her in his wolf form?

He glanced back at the werewolf, who was making his escape down the road on foot. He'd managed to shift back into human form before taking off, which pissed Zane off even more.

He turned his attention back to Skylar and lowered his

nose to her face. He let out a soft growl, hoping she'd wake up and talk to him.

His nose brushed something wet at her temple. His breath caught in his throat as fear seized his body. He licked the wetness.

Blood.

She'd been shot, and there was no fucking way he could help her in his current form.

He lay down by her still body and rested his head on her chest. The slow rise and fall of her breathing gave him some consolation, as did the steady beat of her heart.

For the first time in his life, he felt fucking useless.

He sat back on his haunches lifted his head and let out his frustration as he howled at the full moon.

CHAPTER 30

*S*kylar blinked back the cobwebs and opened her eyes. The starry night sky stared back at her. She frowned for a second, wondering how the hell she'd ended up sprawled on the ground.

Then she remembered.

The attacker.

She tried to sit up, but a heavy weight on her chest pinned her down.

She glanced down. And smiled. She'd know that wolf anywhere.

Zane lifted his furry face off her chest and gazed into her eyes. He leaned forward and gave her a lick across the face.

"Enough. You can get off me now." She eased up onto her elbows as he lifted his head. She winced at the sharp pain in the side of her temple. Reaching up, her fingers brushed something wet.

She held her hand out and frowned at her bloodstained fingers.

"I don't remember hitting my head."

"That's because you didn't. He shot you. The bullet grazed

the side of your head. You're lucky to be alive." Zane's deep voice echoed in the darkness. She looked over in his direction.

He stayed beside her, crouched like a predator, his naked body gleaming under the bright moonlight. She'd been too focused on her injury to realize he'd shifted into his human form.

A cold shiver ran down her spine. Shot? Her body began to shake uncontrollably.

"Holy shit." It was all she could force past her lips. "I didn't realize he had a gun. I thought he was some unarmed crackhead trying to steal my equipment again." She pushed to her feet. Her legs buckled, and Zane was suddenly right there, his strong hands around her waist, holding her up, lending her his strength.

"Easy. Are you all right? Maybe you have a concussion from the fall." His eyes bored into hers with worry. He probed the side of her head with tender fingers as all the breath left her lungs in a whoosh.

"I'm fine. I'm just shaken, that's all." She sucked in a deep breath to steady her runaway heart.

"Skylar, what were you thinking?" He tightened his hold on her waist and glared at her. Even without the blinding headlights from her truck, she still would have been able to tell how pissed off he was by his harsh tone.

"I was thinking I needed to protect my business," she fired back. Her mood shifted, replacing fear with irritation.

"It was a stupid move coming out here by yourself this late at night," he growled.

Anger flared in her veins. She'd been bullied by men throughout her life, and she was fucking sick and tired of it.

She shoved her hands against his steely chest, but he didn't budge.

"You have no idea what it's like trying to run your own

business. You wouldn't understand what it's like to never seem to get ahead." She stuck her finger in the middle of his chest. "Everything you ever had was given to you. Your family, your future, your position in life. Not everyone gets that. Not everyone is born into a family who cares about them. Some of us are born into a shitty family. Some of us were not meant to survive, but end up doing that very thing anyway. Through our hell, we find a purpose and try to find some redemption."

She'd never been so damn mad in her life. Not when her father would forget to feed her when she was five years old. Not when her father would beat the hell out of her when she was eight, for not cooking his dinner to his liking. Not even when her father let his druggie friends fondle her in exchange for some dope when she hit puberty.

"So don't stand there and fucking tell me what to do! You don't have that right. Are we clear?" She hissed out the last words as her hand itched to slap his perfectly handsome face.

His eyes widened and then narrowed before he pulled her hard into his chest. Her body was pressed flush against his, and she could feel her nipples hardening against his chest.

She hated the hold he had on her body and her emotions. And when she should have been afraid of his alpha male routine, she was anything but. Her body warmed under the pressure of his, and she didn't fight the urge to arch against his body like a cat.

Zane Steele was going to be the death of her. That much she knew.

*H*e'd thought she was shot. The second he'd heard the gunshot ring out across the night, the worst possible scenario had exploded in his mind in vivid color.

His heart had stopped in those terrifying few seconds of uncertainty.

When he'd bolted over to her and attacked the asshole that had hurt her, all he had wanted was to taste his blood and rip out his throat. It was her small whimper that had stunned him while the wolf escaped.

He'd never been so relieved and grateful in his entire life. Never.

When he'd laid his head on her chest and felt her breathe, he'd been given hope that she was going to be okay.

Now here she was, alive and full of fire, like always. His Sky.

His body tensed as she rubbed against him like a feral animal, and his dick hardened to the point of pain. All he could think about was taking her right here under the hot Arkansas moon.

He slammed his mouth down across hers, groaning as her sweet taste exploded in his mouth like candy. He cupped her head and angled for a deeper kiss while his other hand slid down to grasp her perfect butt. Working on a construction site had kept her hard and toned in all the right places.

"Zane," she moaned into his mouth as she wrapped her arms around his neck and pulled him closer.

Damn, she was going to make him explode right here if he didn't get inside her soon.

He slid his hands down to her ass and lifted her. Her legs wrapped around his waist as he walked her over to her truck. His hand grazed the door, making sure the metal wouldn't be too hot for her tender flesh before pressing her back against the truck. His erection strained forward, pressing into her flat stomach. He needed desperately to be inside her.

"Now. I want you now," she demanded as she moved her hot mouth to the side of his neck and sucked hard.

"Fuck, Skylar." Jolts of pleasure shot across his balls.

She reached down and unzipped her jeans. He continued to kiss her as she kicked the denim off and reached for her shirt.

He held her head between his palms and searched her face. Desire filled her dilated pupils as her nostrils flared. She was scenting him, smelling his heightened arousal. Disappointment flooded his gut. He still couldn't smell her.

"Are you sure?" He gazed down into her face and prayed that she wasn't going to change her mind. If she did, he was going to find a pond and jump in.

"Yes. Now." She pulled him down for another deep, searching kiss. There was no hesitation in either her eyes or her body.

His fingertips brushed the back of her bra as he fumbled with the hook. When he finally managed to release the article of clothing, he sighed with relief. He was one step closer to finding heaven.

She shrugged out of her white lacy bra and hooked her fingers on either side of her panties and pulled them down over her slim hips.

She kicked them to the side.

He took a step back and clenched his hands to keep from touching her.

Her white skin shimmered under the glow of the full moon. Her hair, red as the desert sun, brushed across her shoulders as she stared back at him with those beautiful eyes. Her pink tongue swiped across her full lips, making his cock harden even more. His gaze dropped to her pretty pink nipples, and his mouth watered for a taste.

She didn't try to cover herself like some untried virgin, yet there was an innocence in her widened gaze that made his heart leap in his chest.

"Why aren't you touching me?" She lifted her chin as if daring him to lie.

"I want to see you, memorize your beauty before I take you. I want you to see me too. I want you to remember how hard I'm going to make you come, and I want it burned inside your head until it's the first thing you think of in the morning and the last thing you think of at night. I don't want you to ever forget, Skylar."

Her lips widened at his coarse language for a brief second before her pupils dilated even further.

"Then come here and show me." Her husky voice left no doubt of her lust for him.

Lust surged through his body and he lifted her in the air. She wrapped her legs around his waist, reminding him how delicious they felt together. Using her thighs, she lifted, nudging his cock against her wet heat.

"I want you in me now." She clutched his shoulders.

She brushed her mouth across his neck, tucked his earlobe into her hot mouth, and nipped.

He growled, fueled by her lust, and reached between their bodies to guide his length into hers.

Poised at her entrance, he met her gaze. She ground down on his cock, burying him deep.

"Oh, god," she cried out as her head fell back. "Don't stop."

"Baby, there's no way I could stop now even if I tried." He tightened his grip on her hips and pressed her against the side of the truck. "It feels too fucking good."

Her muscles clamped down around his dick like velvet heat. She lifted herself up and powered back down on his dick, making his body tremble in anticipation.

He gripped her hips, forcing her to go slow. He covered her mouth with his, kissing her long and deep.

He slid all the way out and then thrust back in, until he was balls deep in paradise. Sweat popped up across his body as he tried to control his own impending orgasm. Her sweet body was making it hard to concentrate on anything but how good her tight pussy felt clamped down around his throbbing cock.

He dipped his head as his mouth closed around her pretty pink nipple and sucked. She clasped his head and held him against her breast.

"That feels so good." She moaned as she writhed against his dick.

"Easy, baby. I want to make you come, but you need to go slow." He sucked harder on the pretty pink bud.

A thin sheen of sweat covered their bodies as their lovemaking turned frenzied.

She whimpered against his mouth and tightened her legs around his waist.

His heart pounded in his head as his balls constricted. He

reached between their bodies and flicked the nubbin between her thighs. She moaned and trembled against him.

"Like that?"

"Yes." She breathed out the word as her eyes glazed over.

He quickened his thrusts inside her tight wet heat. Her moans grew louder in the silence of the night.

"Come for me, Skylar. Come all over my dick," he growled as he pistoned his hips faster.

"Zane," she cried out. Her head dropped back and her body quivered as her climax washed over her. He rode out her orgasm while holding back his own impending pleasure.

"Fuck." He tightened his hold on her body as he buried himself deep. His climax stole over him to the point of stars floating in front of his eyes. He growled as his seed spilled deep within her body. He held her close, refusing to let her go.

They stayed that way, their sweaty bodies clasped together while they struggled to catch their breath.

Sated, he lifted his head and stared down at her.

A satisfied smile crossed her beautiful lips as she stared back at him through heavy-lidded eyes.

"You are a man true to his word, Zane Steele." Her grin deepened.

"Damn right I am." He pressed his lips to hers in a gentle, unhurried motion.

"That's the fastest I've ever climaxed," she whispered, burying her face in the crook of his neck.

He smiled with male satisfaction as he ran a hand up and down her back. Fuck, he loved the way she felt under his touch. It was as if he couldn't get enough of her—how she looked, how she tasted, how she felt.

He shifted his chest against her. Her hard nipples rasped against him and made his dick twitch.

He wanted her again. He couldn't deny that.

But next time, he wanted her in bed, where he could take his time exploring every inch of her glorious body with his fingers and mouth.

She glanced in the direction the attacker had fled. Fear flickered behind her blue eyes.

"Don't worry. He's gone." He cupped her head and brought her into his chest.

"For now. He'll come back." She burrowed into his embrace, and his arms slid around her, cocooning her against him.

The thought of Skylar getting hurt or worse shook him to his very core. He tightened his hold on her, needing the reminder that she was still here, with him and safe.

"And when he does, I'll be here. And next time I'll kill him."

CHAPTER 32

"*I* got breakfast."

Damon frowned as he was awakened from a deep sleep and reached for Ava across the hotel bed, but all he got was air. He sat up and glanced around the hotel room.

No sign of her anywhere.

So who was talking?

"Open up! I've got coffee and doughnuts and everything," Granny's voice called out from the other side of the hotel door.

"Fuck me." Damon growled and whipped the sheet off his bare body. He snagged his jeans off the floor and smiled as he remembered Ava getting down on her knees last night to help him get undressed. She'd stayed there until he'd almost exploded before taking her on the floor.

Buttoning his jeans, he lumbered to the door and peered out the peephole.

Granny had her eye up to the tiny opening as if she could see inside. Shaking his head, he opened the door.

"I've got breakfast," the older woman said brightly. She

pushed her way into the room and set the tray of coffee and bag of doughnuts on the dresser.

"What time is it? And where's Ava?" He glanced out the door into the hallway, but it was empty.

"She's downstairs using the hotel computer. Said she was emailing her contractor today." Granny glanced around the room.

Her gaze landed on Ava's thong hanging on a nearby lampshade. She arched her brow.

Damon snagged a glazed doughnut out of the brown paper bag and shoved half of it in his mouth. He was an adult, but Granny had a way of making him feel like a naughty teenager.

"Go ahead and eat all those." Granny waved her hand at the bag. "Ava already took two and a cup of coffee with her." She grabbed the second Styrofoam cup and popped the lid off. Pulling out some pink packets of sugar substitute and tiny cups of creamer, she doctored her coffee to her liking before tasting the brew.

She eased into the chair by the window and took a sip. "Are you ready for Ava to have her house finished?" She stared up at him with expectant eyes.

"More than ready." He finished off his second doughnut and fished his hand in the bag for another.

"You know, that girl ain't going nowhere." Her eyes danced with mischief.

"I didn't say she was." Damon forced the bit of doughnut down his throat and shifted his weight. He might be mated to the love of his life, but his past and being abandoned rose up in his mind.

"She's the best thing that ever happened to me." He sat the coffee down and walked over to the window.

"Don't give her all the credit, son." Granny stood and patted him on the back. "She's lucky to have you, Damon. I hope you know that. You should know that you are the best thing that happened to her, too." She made her way over to the door. "Granny." Damon turned to face the woman who'd raised him for the better part of his life. They might not be blood-related, but their bond went much deeper, and she was very much his family.

"Yes?"

"I think I'm lucky for all the women in my life." He gave her a respectful nod.

Her weathered face broke out into a wide grin. "I think you're right." She nodded toward the panty-clad lampshade. "You know, if you ordered some of my edible underwear, there would be no evidence of Ava's drawers hanging all over the place."

CHAPTER 33

"*A* headache, clothes reeking of cigarette smoke, and some ugly chick's underwear. That's all I got to show for our little investigative trip to the club last night." Lucien scowled as he lifted his leather-clad arm to his nose and sniffed. "God, I hate cigarette smoke."

"I get the headache and the smoke, but how the fuck did you get some chick's underwear?" Jaxon smirked, then took a sip of his coffee and leaned back in the chair in the back room of the Moon Goddess Tattoo Shop.

"She pulled them off at the bar and stuffed them in the back pocket of my jeans." Lucien's eyes widened in horror. "Dude, she even wrote her number on the crotch."

"So, girls are getting creative with their calling cards." Jaxon nodded his head in appreciation. "I like it. Maybe I should be whipping off my boxers, scrawling my number on the band, and giving them to the next girl I wanna hook up with."

"You don't even wear underwear, dumbass." Lucien shook his head and pulled a pencil off the counter. He used the pencil to pick the thong off the floor and fling it into the nearby wastebasket. He'd been digging in his back pocket for his phone and had pulled out the panties instead. The second he'd realized what he was holding, he had tossed them to the floor like a hot potato.

"You're not that squeamish about thongs." Jaxon snorted.

"You didn't see the girl wearing these. Plus, she smoked." He cocked his head at his partner. "Even you wouldn't have tried to hit that. And you try to tap everything."

"I resent that statement." Jaxon took a sip and shook his head.

"I can't help it if the ladies love me."

"You just wait, asshole. There's going to be one girl who comes along who'll break your heart. You'll be as whipped as Damon, Braxton, and Jayden."

"Don't say that. You'll jinx me or something." Jaxon sat up straight, and his eyes widened.

Lucien shook his head as his cell phone buzzed in his pocket.

He pulled it out and gritted his teeth.

"Fuck, it's Barrett."

"Dude, you've got to talk to him sometime. You can't keep holding him off," Jaxon warned.

Lucien hit the answer button and held the piece of plastic to his ear.

"What's up, boss?" Lucien steeled himself for Barrett's barrage of questions.

"Nice to see you haven't lost your phone. Seems like a lot of my werewolves are in the habit of losing their phones and can't seem to get in contact with me." Barrett's low voice growled across the line.

"Boss, I don't know where Zane is. I'm sure he must be deep undercover if he's not calling you back." Lucien looked down at the counter where Zane's phone sat. He'd talked Matt into parking Zane's Harley in the locked parking lot.

He knew Zane would come back for his Harley, and he wanted it available for him when he did.

Never get between a Were and his Harley.

"What's your location?" Barrett thundered.

"The Moon Goddess."

"I find it ironic that you just so happen to be at the last place Zane was actually seen before he apparently up and disappeared without letting his Pack Master know where he was going."

Lucien flinched. "I'm sure whatever is going on with Zane is . . . temporary."

"*Temporary*. Sounds like a perfect word to describe his future status as a Guardian."

The call ended before Lucien could say another word.

"How bad was it?" Jaxon looked as if he was bracing himself for bad news.

"Let's just say if we don't find Zane and find him quick, then he's no longer going to be part of the Guardian team."

CHAPTER 34

Zane woke up in bed with Skylar's naked body pressed against him. A smile grew on his lips, and he ran his fingertips down her slender back, loving how she felt under his touch.

After they'd made it home, he'd carried her straight to bed. After doctoring her head wound, they had made love two more times before she'd drifted off to sleep, sated and content.

His dick stiffened and lust licked deep in his stomach. He wanted her again. He couldn't help himself. She was irresistible.

She moaned in her sleep and turned over. He wrapped his arm around her waist and tugged her into his chest. His erection prodded at her entrance.

His fingers found her nipple, and he teased the bud. A soft moan slipped past her lips.

"I like the way you wake a girl up." Skylar's husky voice made his dick pulse with lust.

"I've actually never woken up with a girl in bed before."

He kissed the pink shell of her ear and rubbed his dick between her thighs. She was wet and ready for him.

"Really? You always kick them out before morning?" She chuckled.

"I've never had a woman stay after sex." He moved his mouth to the crook of her neck and nuzzled her soft flesh. What he wouldn't give to smell her desire for him. She stiffened in his arms and looked over her shoulder at him.

"What?" He frowned.

"You've never spent the night with a woman?"

"No. I've never wanted to before." He dipped his head and captured her bottom lip between his teeth and growled.

*H*er heart squeezed in her chest at his words.

Zane had never woken up next to a woman before? She'd known he wasn't a virgin, not by a long shot. By the way he knew how to move his body and the miraculous things he could do with his tongue, she knew he was no novice. "I'm stunned."

"Not the reaction I was hoping for. I'd rather have you breathless and screaming my name." He grinned as he dipped his head and sucked a nipple into his hot mouth.

Her breath caught in her throat as her body warmed with desire. She rubbed her legs together to quell the ache he'd awakened.

"I didn't scream your name last night?" She struggled to concentrate on her words as lust swept through her body.

"Actually, you did—many, many times." He moved his attention to her other breast.

She turned over to face him. She wanted to look into his eyes as he slid inside her body. She wanted—no, needed—this connection. She'd never had that before. Someone kind and gentle yet able to control her body and give her what she needed when even she didn't know what that was.

She pressed her palm to his chest and froze as she met his gaze.

"What's wrong?" He frowned down at her, his eyes glowing yellow.

"How do you feel?" she whispered. The other time she'd been this close to a Were when he'd shifted, it had been horrifying.

"Horny. How do you feel?" He cocked his head.

"Zane, your eyes." The words slipped out as she tensed.

His eyes widened in horror. He shoved himself away from her and jumped off the bed, putting distance between them. He glanced at the mirror and then clenched his hands.

Forgetting her nakedness, she rose up to her knees and reached for him. "Zane."

His gaze swept across her body, and his nostrils flared. His muscles tensed as he seemed to struggle not to touch her.

She grabbed the sheet, tugged it around her body, and stood. With her heart pounding in her chest, she took a step forward.

"Don't touch me. I don't have any control, Skylar. I don't want to hurt you." He stepped away and squeezed his eyes shut.

"Even as a werewolf, I doubt you would hurt me." She spoke softly.

"Are you fucking serious?" He shot her a heated glare. "Skylar, I have no control over my body anymore, and if I don't find a way to cure it, I'm as good as gone."

"What do you mean?" She frowned. Was he sicker than he was letting on?

"What do you think is going to happen when I shift in front of humans? That crime is punishable by death."

"Yeah, but you are a high-ranked Guardian. They won't punish you for something you can't control."

"Yeah? How am I going to prove that I can't control it? Is there some kind of werewolf test you can buy at the fucking drug store where you can pee on a stick?" he growled.

Irritation flared in her gut, and she fought to keep her temper under control.

"I get that you are frustrated about your condition, but you have no right to talk to me like I'm an idiot."

"Then get your head out of your ass and understand what's going on." He slammed his fist on her dresser. The wood cracked and splintered.

"You need to back that shit up right now, Zane Steele. You may be a male, but I'm not going to stand here and take your shit. Are we clear?" Her body trembled under her anger, and she wanted nothing better than to knock him on his ass.

And it was looking like she was going to get her chance.

CHAPTER 36

A low growl rumbled out of his throat as he threw his head back and squeezed his eyes shut. His mind was fighting with his body to control his shift, but it was a battle he was quickly losing.

Sweat popped out across his body as his muscles strained to accommodate his new form. He fell to his knees, adrenaline coursing through him, fueling his transition into wolf. His muscles stretched and lengthened as his tendons shifted into his new body.

Why the fuck couldn't he control his own goddamn body? He couldn't continue to live this way. He wouldn't.

He lifted his head and opened his eyes, hoping Skylar had the sense to take off before he could hurt her.

"Zane."

He jerked his head to the corner of the room, where she was standing like a goddess in nothing but that damn sheet wrapped around her. Her beautiful red hair hung like satin curtains to her shoulders, and her blue eyes met his.

He growled, showing off his teeth and hoping she would get the hint and run like hell.

She dropped to one knee and held out her hand. "I know you won't hurt me. I trust you."

Rage and anger pulsed through his body. The urge to taste blood swamped him. How the hell was he not going to hurt her? He had lost all his control. Why didn't she understand?

He squeezed his eyes shut, trying to force the shift back into human.

But his body couldn't be controlled. He couldn't be controlled. Opening his eyes, he saw his target. And pounced.

CHAPTER 37

Skylar had braced herself, hoping that any minute Zane was going to snap out of it and shift back into his human form. Or at best, be able to control his anger in wolf form.

She knew she had figured wrong the second his eyes popped open and his pupils dilated. The only thing she could do now was brace herself for the attack.

He pounced and shoved her to the floor, and his massive body pinned her down. She sucked in a breath at the impact. His hot breath was inches away from her neck as he growled low and deadly.

Bloodlust. He wanted blood. He wanted her blood.

The realization had her frantically searching for some object on the floor with which to defend herself. A shoebox sat a foot away from her face.

She never bought shoes, and she sure as hell couldn't remember what she'd put inside this particular box. Hopefully something heavy, like a brick.

She reached out and grabbed the box with one hand.

Surprisingly, it was pretty heavy. Her fingers found the

top and she tried to pry open the lid, but it wasn't budging. It was tied down with some twine.

Zane lifted his head back and growled, and she knew what was coming next. He was going to rip her throat out. She'd been around alpha males enough to know the drill. Once they were set on bloodlust, nothing would satisfy them. They needed the taste. Craved it.

Grasping the shoebox in her hand, she brought it down hard across Zane's furry head. He fell off her and collapsed in a heap on the floor.

"Oh, shit. I killed him." Her heart dropped to her toes. "Please God, tell me I didn't kill him."

A tear escaped from behind her eyes and rolled down her cheek. Forgetting her sheet, she crawled over to his lifeless body and laid her head on his chest.

He was so very still.

She held her breath as she waited for his heart to beat.

When she felt the strong, steady beat against her cheek, she let tears fall freely.

Lying down beside him, she sobbed into his furry body.

"*I* like this one, Ava." Granny pointed to the painting in shades of green and yellow and gray that hung along the brick wall of Ande Allison's art studio. "It reminds me of coming home again."

"It reminds me of a hot summer day and lying naked in the grass." Ava nodded and turned to Damon. "Damon, what does this remind you of?"

"It reminds me that I need to be working on a mission for Barrett instead of wandering around some artsy-fartsy studio." He scowled and placed his hands on his hips.

"But I want to get some art for our home." Ava pouted and snuggled up to him.

Damn, he was always a goner whenever she touched him.

"I didn't say you couldn't get any. I just don't think I need to be here with you." He traced a finger down her cheek.

"I want you here with me." She slid her arms around his neck and smiled up at him.

He pulled her tighter into his embrace, once again struck by the reality that she was all his.

"I know, baby, but I have a job I need to do."

"What kind of work do you do, Mr. Trahan?" Ande Allison, the artist and proprietor, shot him a friendly smile.

"You could say I'm in the protection business." He cut his eyes at the petite blonde.

"Oh, like a bodyguard. How exciting." Her smile brightened.

Ava snorted and shook her head before slipping out of his arms. "Ande, I think I want to take those two over there. I know just the place to hang them."

"Perfect. I'll get them ready for you." The artist began taking down the artwork.

"I like this one too," Granny announced from the other side of the room. "It reminds me of something familiar."

Damon followed Ava over to where Granny was standing.

Damon snorted as his gaze fell upon the picture that was leaning up against the wall.

"It's something you haven't seen in about fifty years," Damon said as he took in the painting that clearly resembled a three-foot penis.

"Granny, are you sure you want that one?" Ava cut her eyes at Damon.

"Of course, dear. Why wouldn't I?"

"'Cause it looks like a dick." Damon barked out a laugh.

"Damon." Ava jabbed him in the ribs.

"Oh, dear." Ande hurried over to them and gave them an apologetic smile. He didn't miss how the blush stole over her cheeks.

"I'm afraid that's not for sale. You see, one of my students did that, and it didn't turn out quite like it was supposed to." The blush darkened.

"Was it supposed to be a dick?" Damon asked.

Ava jabbed him hard in the side.

"I think she was trying to paint a tree." Ande put her arm

around Granny and tried to herd the old lady away. But Granny wasn't having it. She shrugged out of the woman's grip and shook her head.

"But I'm interested in purchasing this piece." Granny pursed her lips and continued to gaze upon the painting.

"I'm sorry, but I really can't sell it." Ande nibbled on her bottom lip as she looked to Ava for help.

"You don't want that, Granny," Damon offered. The last thing the woman needed was a picture of a giant dick hanging over her dining room table. Thanksgiving would never be the same again. "Besides, it belongs to her student, and she can't legally sell something that doesn't belong to her."

"Fine." Granny pursed her wrinkled lips and gave Ande a stern look that would make most humans back down. But to her credit, Ande didn't budge. She just stood there with a cheery smile on her face.

"I do have something in the back you might like. You did say you were from Louisiana?"

"That's right." Granny cocked her head, clearly interested in what the artist had that might pique her interest.

"I'll be right back."

A few seconds later, Ande returned with a sizeable canvas and leaned it against the brick wall. Abstract bright red and fuchsia swirls and slashes of green were painted behind what appeared to be an abstract black wrought-iron fence.

"It's beautiful. And it reminds me of one of the gardens in the Garden District of New Orleans." Granny's wide smile stretched her wrinkles to the corners.

"That's where I got my inspiration." Ande clasped her hands together as a look of unabashed pleasure crossed he face. "I stayed at a B&B there on my last trip to New Orleans."

"It's perfect. I'll take this instead." Granny pulled her wallet out of her white plastic purse.

"I'll wrap it for you so it won't get damaged."

Damon sighed and glanced at his Luminox watch again.

"What's with you, anyway?" Ava came up behind him and wrapped her arms around his waist. Her small, pert breasts pressed into his back, eliciting a reaction from his body.

"Nothing. Art isn't my thing. You know that, Ava." He turned, pulling her into his embrace.

She looked up and narrowed her astute eyes at him. "You're not just here on a visit, are you? Did Barrett send you here on a mission?"

He pressed his lips together in a thin line, warning her not to say anything, especially around Granny. The last thing he needed was her interference while on a recon mission for his Pack Master.

"Ava..." He warned.

"I know, I know. You can't tell me." She pouted.

"That's right. You knew what you were getting into when you mated me." He grinned and pressed his lips to hers in a heated kiss.

Her lips parted, and he didn't miss his chance to taste her sweet mouth. He groaned as he dipped his tongue between her lips while holding her snug against his body. Her hands slid up his bare arms and laced together behind his neck, pulling him further into the kiss. His body began to ache with that familiar need that always grew when she was in his arms.

Nothing ever felt as good as his Ava. Nothing.

"Ahem." Granny cleared her throat behind him.

Reluctantly, he pulled away from his mate and faced the older woman.

"Now, now. You two need to have better manners than to

be making out like two rats in a wool sock. Why, Mrs. Allison is going to think I've raised a wild animal."

Ava barked out a laugh at the ironic meaning while he gave Granny a smile. "No one would think that, Granny."

"They better not. I've got a reputation to protect, you know." She hiked her white purse up on her shoulder and nodded at him to take the canvases the artist had wrapped for them.

"Thank you so much. I hope you'll enjoy your new pieces." Ande handed the canvases to Damon and smiled.

He breathed out a sigh of relief as they made their way out the door. One day at the gallery was enough to last him a lifetime.

CHAPTER 39

*P*ain seared his head as Zane blinked his eyes open and stared up at the white, bumpy ceiling.

He held up his hand.

He'd shifted back to his human form while he had been unconscious.

Wincing, he glanced down at the heavy weight that was pressed against his chest. A ghost of a smile crossed his lips when he saw Skylar's dark red locks spilled out across his skin. Her slender shoulders were shaking as tears slid down her face and landed on his naked chest.

He cupped the back of her head. "Skylar." Her head jerked up, and she met his gaze.

"Oh, my god. I thought I'd killed you. And then I saw you were breathing and I thought maybe you had brain damage because you wouldn't wake up. You've been out all day." She buried her face in the crook of his neck and clung to him like a vine.

"Nope. No damage." He winced as another pain shot through his skull. He rubbed the side of his head. "What did you have in that box anyway? A brick?"

"No. Rocks," she said pitifully.

"Of course. What else would be in a shoebox?" He wanted to laugh, but it hurt too fucking bad.

She pulled away and met his gaze. Her lip quivered as she stared at him, so very serious. "Sophia gave it to me. She collects rocks, and she wanted me to have a collection too."

He eased up on his elbows and glanced down at his nudity. Skylar glanced at his erection, and her face turned a pretty shade of pink. She looked away as she tried to continue her conversation.

"Who's Sophia?"

"A very special friend." Skylar gave him a true smile.

Whoever Sophia was made Skylar happy. He was glad she had a friend she could count on. Although he did wonder about a grown-ass woman collecting rocks. Seemed kind of juvenile.

To each her own.

He got his feet under him while Skylar kept her arm around his waist to steady him. He didn't bother telling her that there was no way she could bear his weight if he did fall —he liked the way she felt against him too much to say anything.

He ambled into the living room and eased himself onto the couch. While he didn't feel any blood coursing down the side of his head, he knew that it was probably bruised at best. He glanced out the window into the darkness. She must have hit him pretty hard to make him lose consciousness for almost twelve hours.

"You know how to handle yourself, I'll give you that." He cracked a smile.

"God, Zane, I'm so sorry. It was just—you had bloodlust in your eyes, and it was like you couldn't even see me..."

He cupped a hand under her chin. His thumb grazed the bottom of her full lip as he searched her face. "Don't be sorry.

You did what you needed to do. I'm the one who needs to apologize."

His chest ached with remorse. He could have killed her. And he wouldn't have remembered any of it.

"I'm so sorry, Skylar. While I'm like this, and unable to control my shift or my actions, I am a danger to you." He stood and shook his head and looked around her apartment. "I can't stop ruining the clothes you get me, but I can't stay here."

He hated this. He hated not having any kind of damn control over anything. He lived his life by the code of the Pack, and he'd strived his whole life to keep his body in control and under discipline.

Hell, control and discipline were what made him a good soldier. That was what made him a hell of a Guardian.

"You can't leave." She jumped to her feet. "Where the hell are you going to go? Someone is going to see you shift, and then where will you be?" Her eyes widened with each word.

"If there's a risk that I can lose control and hurt you, then I can't stay here. You know that." His words came out harsher than he meant them to, but his gut was still twisting with what could have happened if Skylar hadn't knocked him out.

"I can handle myself. You said so yourself. You don't need to worry about me." She stuck her hands in her jeans pockets and lifted her chin in that defiant way she'd had as a child.

"I could never live with myself if I hurt you, if something happened to you. Don't you understand?" He grabbed her arms and gave her a little shake, hoping the gravity of the situation would sink into that thick skull of hers.

"Don't do that. You don't tell me what to do." She wrenched free of his hold and took a step back while piercing him with a glare.

"Stop being so unreasonable. You know as well as I do that if I lost control, I could hurt you."

"And you know that I can handle myself. Believe me, I've had to do that since I was a child."

"This is different. This is dangerous."

"What did you think my childhood consisted of? Puppies and cartoons?" She curled her fingers into fists and leaned into his space. "By the time I was old enough to walk, I knew I had to find places to hide to keep my father from hitting me when he got drunk. By the time I was in school, I knew enough to stay out of his way and hide the food I managed to take from your house under my bed so I wouldn't go days without eating. And when I hit puberty and started looking like a young woman, I had to learn how to hit back hard enough so I wouldn't be raped by my father's friends. So don't you sit there and tell me I'm some helpless female when it comes to out-of-control werewolves who don't give a shit about anyone but themselves." Chest heaving and eyes flashing with anger, she spun on her heel and headed into the bathroom.

Zane felt like he'd been hit in the chest by a two-by-four.

He'd known her life had not been easy, but never in a million years would he have guessed she was physically abused.

Anger flooded his body like lava in a volcano. The image of her piece-of-shit father trying to hit her—or even worse, letting his friends try to lay their hands on her—had rage flooding through his body.

He was quickly losing control, and he didn't fucking care anymore. He lifted his head back and growled as the shift began to take over his body. He wanted nothing more than to seek out her offenders and rip them apart with his teeth until they were nothing but a bloody smear on the ground.

CHAPTER 40

*T*he bathroom door flew open and Skylar came barreling out as a loud roar echoed through the small apartment.

"Zane, what the hell are you doing? Keep it down, or nosy old Mrs. Nelson is going to call the cops!" she hissed at him. He once again shifted into wolf form and began pacing the tiny living room floor. He would make it two steps before turning around. He looked more like a caged tiger than a werewolf.

"The last thing I need is her interference." She didn't have time to look for another apartment, and she doubted she could find one as cheap as this one. Every spare cent went into her business. She wanted to keep a low profile, get her business on solid footing, and get her project going for girls who needed a safe place to stay.

That was her priority, and now Zane was going to ruin everything with his whole alpha male routine.

Knock, knock, knock.

She stiffened, and Zane stopped his pacing. Maybe if they stayed quiet, whoever it was would go away.

Knock, knock, knock.

She shot him a glare when she saw that wasn't happening.

"Go in the bedroom and stay there," she whispered.

He didn't move for a few seconds, and she wondered if she was going to have to grab him by his hairy tail and drag him.

He stared at her through intense, wolfy eyes, and she fought the tiny shiver of fear that zinged through her stomach at the memory of what had happened the last time he shifted.

She didn't want to hurt him, nor did she want to draw attention to herself by having him here.

"Please," she implored.

He gave a low growl and lumbered back into the bedroom. She closed the door behind him.

She grabbed the remote control off the small table by the couch and turned on the stereo system.

Glad she'd put her robe on, she slowly walked to the door and pressed her sweaty palms to her thighs before reaching for the doorknob.

Easing open the door, she blinked in surprise.

"Hector, what are you doing here?" He was standing there holding his daughter, Sophia, in his arms. Skylar looked over his shoulder as Mrs. Nelson popped her head out her own door, scowled, and slammed it shut.

Thank god the old woman didn't want to talk.

"What the hell is going on in there?" He cocked his head and looked around her.

"Just listening to the radio, that's all," she said a little too quickly. She held her breath, hoping he wouldn't ask to come inside. She wasn't sure how Zane was going to react to another male in her apartment.

"Look, Maria is in labor, and I need Sophia to stay with you tonight." He gave her a wide-eyed, frantic stare as she

139

sleepy-eyed child raised her head off his shoulder and held her arms up for Skylar to take her.

Her heart tugged as she took Sophia in her arms. The little girl laid her head back on her shoulder.

"Where are your other kids?" She looked out behind him to make sure they were not in tow, but he was alone.

"They are at the neighbor's house. I couldn't leave Sophia there because she's allergic to the neighbor's cat. The last time she went over there, she had hives for a week." His breathing grew more rapid.

"What about dogs? Is she allergic to dogs?" Zane had probably shed enough to make a coat. She didn't need Sophia to have a reaction to that as well.

"No, just cats." Hector shook his head. "Look, Skylar, I understand this is really bad timing, but I don't have anyone else I can call." He pressed a small pink princess backpack in her hand and began backing away.

"I'll be back tomorrow to pick her up. My mother is driving in from Louisiana to stay with the kids. He jogged to his truck and called out before jumping into the driver's seat, "I owe you one, boss." With a wave of his hand, he cranked up the old truck, backed out of the parking space, and tore out of the parking lot. "Skylar, I'm tired." Sophia wrapped her arms tighter around Skylar's neck and settled against her shoulder.

She couldn't help but smile, and she patted the child's tiny back. Her fingers brushed the soft cotton pajamas that were the color of cotton candy. She stepped inside and shut the door.

"Doggie," Sophia said in her sleepy voice as she raised her head and looked over Skylar's shoulder.

She spun around. Zane stood in the middle of the open bedroom doorway.

"How did you get out?" Her eyes widened.

He cocked his head to the side and stared at Sophia in her arms.

"Shit." She slammed a hand over her mouth. She never cursed, and certainly not in front of children. But Zane made her do a lot of things she didn't normally do.

"Skylar said a bad word."

"I know, sweetie. I'm sorry." She tightened her hold on the little girl. She might care for Zane, but she sure as hell wasn't going to let him hurt Sophia.

"Doggie." Apparently, Skylar's bad language was quickly forgotten as Sophia turned back to Zane. She tried to wiggle out her other arm to reach for the animal, but Skylar tightened her hold on the child.

"Doggie," Sophia whimpered.

Skylar met his wolf's gaze and narrowed her eyes. "Don't you dare think about touching her."

Much to her surprise, he lowered his head and then curled up on the floor, all the while keeping his eyes on them both.

His eyes no longer glinted yellow, promising bloodlust. Instead, they were his normal blue color.

She slowly turned so Sophia could look at the "doggie."

He rested his long snout between his outstretched paws. His dark fur ruffled a little as the air conditioner vent overhead circulated the cool air. He held her gaze, only breaking his stare to blink. His chest rose and fell in an even rhythm, one she'd not seen when he'd shifted before. Odd. Usually he was on edge, angry, and dangerous. But now, he looked as if he could control his emotions a bit better.

"Zane." She spoke his name quietly and stepped closer. Right now, he was between her and the bedroom door. She needed to get Sophia to bed, and she didn't intend on spending the night on the couch with a four-year-old. She had too much work she needed to get done tomorrow since she was a day behind.

"I need you to move so we can get to bed."

Zane lifted his head and squinted at her. Her heart stumbled to a halt in her chest, and she forced herself to suck in deep breaths. Just getting upset and showing fear was the worst possible thing she could do right now.

"Move," she repeated and hugged Sophia close to her chest.

A low rumble came from behind his closed lips, yet he didn't show his teeth. He looked like he was pissed at having to move his large body out of the way.

Slowly he got to his feet and let out a sigh like she was inconveniencing him. He padded over to a corner, walked out a circle, and lay down.

She arched an eyebrow and waited a few seconds before heading into the bedroom and shutting the door behind her. She reached out to turn the lock on the doorknob. Her fingers brushed across something wet.

"So that's how he opened the door. With his mouth." She wiped her hand on her robe as she walked over to the bed. Pulling down the comforter, she placed Sophia in the soft bed and tucked her in.

"I'll be right back." She brushed the hair out of the child's face as her eyelids fluttered closed.

She turned on the faucet and made quick work of brushing her teeth. She peeked her head around the corner to make sure Sophia hadn't gotten up.

A smile lit her face as she watched the little girl sleep deeply. Her arms were stretched over her head and her pouty lips were slightly parted. Her pink pajamas were hiked up, showing off her chubby stomach.

She tiptoed in the room and carefully opened a drawer and pulled out an old T-shirt and some shorts. She didn't usually sleep in anything, but with Sophia here and Zane in the next room, tonight called for clothing.

After donning the T-shirt and shorts, Skylar slipped between the covers, careful not to wake her little bed partner. Out in the distance, the first peals of thunder echoed and a brief flash of lightning slashed across the sky.

Skylar settled into the bed and smiled with the promise of rain. At least it was going to be a good night to sleep. After today's events, she needed it.

CHAPTER 41

ane woke to booming thunder that rattled the tiny windows of the apartment. He sat up and frowned at his nakedness.

Easing up off the floor, he looked around. His gaze landed on a green bag sitting on the edge of the kitchen counter. He remembered Skylar bitching about having to buy him clothes.

Another round of thunder echoed outside.

Despite her own hectic schedule, she always seemed to be anticipating what he would need next. She was fluidity to his discipline.

He opened the bag and pulled out a white T-shirt with an eighties band scrawled across the front, then a pair of jeans. They were just his size. At least he didn't have to replace the boots she'd bought him earlier. That was the one thing he never ruined when he shifted.

He pulled on the jeans, smirking as he realized she didn't buy him any underwear. Maybe it was a subconscious thought on her part.

Lightning stretched across the sky like claws.

He ambled over to the window and pulled back the flimsy white curtain. Resting his hand on the top of the windowsill, he gazed out at the summer storm rolling in.

The parking lot was half full and all the other tenants' windows were dark. The only light was the lightning in the bleak sky. He glanced over at the clock on the microwave and noted the time. Two a.m.

It would be light in a few hours. And once that sun came up, he was going to have to leave. He needed to find the cure to whatever was preventing him from controlling his shift.

Pushing away from the window, he sunk onto the couch. It was too short for him to be able to stretch out, but if he bent his knees, he should be able to sleep in that position.

He'd slept in worse conditions than this.

Hell, at least he was inside and out of the weather.

CHAPTER 42

*S*kylar yawned and stretched out in the bed as the light of dawn sparkled through her window. She glanced over and noted the sky was bright and clear, with no evidence of last night's rain.

She turned over to check on Sophia. Her heart stuttered to a standstill when she saw the bed was empty.

She jumped out of bed and threw open the bedroom door. She made it only a few steps before she froze at what she saw on the couch.

Zane had shifted back into his human form and was lying on his back on the couch. Little Sophia was lying sprawled on his bare chest, and he had his arm draped over her back, making sure she wouldn't fall.

Her heart and her womb lurched at the tender sight.

She let a sigh slip past her lips as she brushed her hand over her heart.

Zane stirred and blinked awake. He glanced down at the child in his arms and then up at her.

"Morning." His hoarse voice had her stomach turning warm with desire.

She cleared her throat and nodded toward the precious package he was holding.

"How did she end up here?" Her gaze flitted back to his sleepy eyes.

"Not sure. She came out during the night when the thunder got bad. She must have thought I was her dad, 'cause the next thing I knew, she'd crawled up on me like a ladder and laid down." He tried to shrug from his reclining position. "I didn't want to disturb her so I let her sleep."

"Oh." She swallowed. Her throat was like sandpaper while her other parts were heating up.

"When did you, ya know"—she waved her hand at him —"shift back?"

"Around two." He wrapped both arms around Sophia's tiny back and sat up. His muscles clenched and strained with the motion in a beautiful dance.

He stood with her still in his arms. Barefoot and dressed only in jeans, he looked like something out of a woman's fantasy.

"Where are you going?" she managed to squeak out when he walked past her.

"I'm putting her in the bed," he whispered over the child's shoulder.

He might be a Guardian, but he knew how to handle a lady, no matter what her age.

She smiled as he gave her his back and walked into the bedroom. She followed behind, watching him gently lay the child down and pull the sheet up to her chin. Sophia mumbled something in her sleep and turned over to the side. He turned and shot her a glare. "What?" "You look like a natural." She grinned.

"Don't let your womb get all weepy. The kid was scared of the thunder and thought I was her dad. It's not personal." He shifted his weight and stuck in hands in his jeans pockets.

"I never thought you would be so good with a little girl. Growing up, you seemed so distant. So aloof."

"I didn't have time to be bugged by little kids like you and my sister." He padded toward the kitchen. "Want some coffee?"

"Sure. I was just about to make some." She brushed past him, trying to calm her heartbeat. How was it he could still smell so freaking good without even having a shower? Totally wasn't fair.

She pulled out the coffee filters from the top cabinet along with the canister of coffee. She busied herself setting up the coffee pot for brewing. She sighed at the pungent scent of the ground beans. She was going to need a lot of caffeine to get through the day.

The coffee sputtered and began spilling into the carafe. She pulled out two large coffee mugs with big blue flowers and placed them on the counter beside the coffee pot. Reaching in the refrigerator, she tugged out the creamer and set it on the counter.

Once the carafe had enough brewed coffee for one, she poured a cup of coffee and handed it to him.

"No. You take it." He gently shoved it back into her hands. "I can wait."

"Thanks." She frowned. Never in her life had anyone put her first. Certainly no male. But Zane treated her differently, like she was more than a pair of boobs in work boots.

Shaking off the silly, nostalgic feeling, she turned her attention back to doctoring her coffee with a liberal amount of creamer. Then she retrieved a canister from the cabinets and cut her eyes at him as she opened the lid.

He narrowed his eyes at her as she spooned a heap of dark powder into her coffee.

"Is that what I think it is?" He cocked his head.

She could feel the censure pouring off him in waves.

She'd taken precautions for years to keep her identity hidden. She just wanted to blend in, be normal. If that meant not shifting then so be it.

"The red wolves don't have a reputation for being greeted warmly by the rest of the wolves in Arkansas. I really don't blame them. Our kind has been a pain in the ass. I'd rather continue to take precautions to keep from shifting than be placed in a category with them. The less that other wolves know about me, the better."

She met his gaze and took a sip. "There's no harm in that is there?"

She waited a beat to hear a lecture from him about denying what she was. But it never came. His gaze softened as if he understood her reasons.

"So what's up with the kid?" He nodded toward the bedroom as he rested a lean hip against the kitchen counter.

"She's the daughter of one of my construction workers, Hector. He was in a tight spot last night and needed me to babysit." She shrugged and took a sip of her coffee. The hot liquid slid down her throat with comforting warmth. She could always count on coffee.

"Anything going on between you two?" He scowled and flexed the muscles in his arms.

She barked out a laugh. "With Hector? He's married with a brood of kids. He had to drop Sophia off because his wife, Maria, went into labor."

"Oh." He relaxed back against the counter. The stress lines around his eyes disappeared.

"Hector's been working with me since I started the business.

He's always on time, he's gotten me more workers, and he's loyal. His wife is a doll. She's always inviting me over for dinner and trying to fatten me up." Skylar laughed, thinking back to the last dinner she'd shared with the family. Maria had told Skylar that men liked women with some meat on their bones before shoving another piece of blueberry cheesecake at her.

The coffee pot had stuttered to a stop. She pulled out the carafe and filled his mug.

"Creamer or sugar?" She glanced up at him.

"No. Just black."

"Ah, like your heart," she joked.

"Smartass." He accepted the hot mug and took a sip. "Good coffee."

"Thanks. I like it strong." "Like sex." He smirked.

Her face heated.

"Shush. You can't talk about that. Sophia's in the other room." She slugged him in the arm.

"She's asleep. Besides, I doubt she knows what we are taking about." He chuckled.

"You never know. The last time she came to the construction site, she picked up a dirty word from one of the workers. Her dad didn't let me forget it, either."

"What did she say?"

"'Shit.' And she repeated it at preschool." Zane barked out a laugh.

"Hector blamed me for it when he got the phone call from the school. She didn't even hear it from me." She scowled at his grin. "It's not funny."

"It kind of is. I can't imagine that little bit saying anything so bad." His eyes sparkled as a slow grin teased the corners of his lips. His gaze dipped to her thighs. She'd forgotten about the tight, skimpy shorts she'd slept in last night. "So what's your plan for today?" She tugged her shirt down, but there was no way it was going to cover her stomach.

"I need to go get my Harley." His eyes narrowed a little, and he looked away.

"Where is it?"

"At the Moon Goddess."

"Do you think it's still there?" She knew the shop well. It was off Main Street and the college crowd liked to frequent the place to get their first tattoo after drinking too much. Even a few of her workers had gotten their arms inked there. She knew there wasn't much parking available and if he'd left his bike there, there was a strong possibility that it had been towed.

"It's still there. Matt is the artist for the Guardians. Since I didn't return, he would have moved it to the gated area in the back."

"So the Guardians get their tatts here? I didn't know that." She took another sip and glanced at his back when he turned to refill his mug. The signature black wings and eyes that spanned his back were impressive. The wings were jagged, and there was nothing serene about them as they arced across his back. Then there were the eyes that peered out between the wings as if they were watching her. The tattoo was intimidating.

"Yep. The same family has done it for generations." He turned around and faced her before taking another sip.

"Always in Jonesboro? I would think they would have someone in Little Rock do it since it's near the Guardian base."

He shook his head. "The council and Pack Master wanted it away from the base. Jonesboro is far enough away but close enough to drive to in a few hours." He took another sip. "Jonesboro is small enough to seem inconspicuous and large enough that we don't draw too much interest when we ride into town."

"I'm sure you draw a lot of interest, from the college girls in particular." She smirked. She could only imagine how gorgeous he looked riding into town on his Harley Davidson. She'd never seen a Guardian who didn't look like a cover model for a magazine. Their sexual appeal alone made them a target for every hot-blooded woman within a hundred-mile radius.

Her stomach knotted as she thought about how many women he'd already been with. Probably thousands.

"I don't have time to entertain little girls and their fantasies. My job comes first."

The little knot in her stomach relaxed. Maybe the number was in the hundreds instead of the thousands.

Didn't make her feel much better.

She ran her fingers through her hair and set her coffee cup down. She had a thousand things to do today, from checking on her construction site to seeing how Maria was doing. She didn't need to be thinking about Zane's many conquests as well.

"I need you to drive me to the Moon Goddess." His rough voice shook her out of her mental fog.

"I've got to run by the hospital to check in and see what's going on with the babysitting situation. The grandmother should be getting into town today so I can drop Sophia off and then take you over to get your bike before going to the construction site."

"Sounds good. Why don't you go ahead and get in the shower? I'll start breakfast and then maybe little bit will be up by the time you get out." His muscles rippled as he bent to take a skillet out from a cabinet. He moved easily about the kitchen, pulling out eggs and bacon from the fridge and getting plates together. He was clearly comfortable in a kitchen. To her it was an odd sight.

"What?" He frowned when he caught her looking at him.

"I just didn't expect you to know how to cook. I know growing up, your family had a maid." The Steele family's housekeeper made no bones about how she felt about Skylar.

She'd made it clear to the Steeles that Skylar was beneath them, and that Katy shouldn't be playing with her.

"You mean Hildie?" He snorted. "She cleaned, but she never once set foot in the kitchen. My mom didn't like anyone in her kitchen. It was her domain." He smiled with genuine affection.

"I didn't know that. I thought your mom was always too busy with running charities and looking after you guys. I just assumed she didn't have time to cook."

"My mom made time for the things that mattered. She always told me that family came first, before anything else." He cracked the egg against the corner of the counter and spilled the yellow, oozy contents into the small bowl he'd retrieved from the cabinet. He cracked several more before dipping a fork into the mixture and whisking until the eggs were beaten and frothy.

Skylar nodded. "Your mom was a very smart woman." Her first memory of being shown kindness was from Victoria Steele. She didn't think she would ever forget the woman.

"Yes, she is." He cut his eyes at her. "She asked Katy about you throughout the years. She wanted to know how you were doing."

"Really?" A twinge of guilt assaulted her gut. She should have kept in touch with his mom—at least she could have sent a letter or taken the time to make a phone call. But she hadn't been sure how it would be received, and she hadn't wanted to bother the woman.

"Yes. She always knew you were going to be successful in whatever you put your mind to." He grinned. "And now look at you. You have your own construction company. That's something to be proud of."

"Thank you." She meant it. It felt good to hear him say

that. "I've thought about her too. About your whole family," she admitted.

He stopped what he was doing and turned to face her. "Really? Did you think about me?" He took a step closer and brushed a stray hair out of her eyes.

Her breath hitched in the back of her throat as her heart thudded so loudly she was sure he could hear every beat.

His spicy male scent washed over her, beckoning her to lean closer. She didn't fight it. It was like being drawn to the sun, knowing it was going to burn once you touched it but being unable to help yourself.

"Maybe," she whispered.

"Maybe? That doesn't sound very convincing." His stepped closer and lifted a strand of her hair, teasing it between two fingers. "Of course I thought about you. You were part of my life when I was little."

A slow, wicked smile touched the corners of his lips and spread across his mouth. Her stomach heated as her gaze focused on those lips and the pleasure he could give.

"What about after you grew up? You're not a little girl anymore, Skylar. Did you think about me then?"

She met his heated gaze and grabbed the hand that kept teasing that strand beside her cheek.

"Yeah. I did. I thought about you a lot Zane," she admitted. "Hmmm." His groan was dark and guttural, and it made her want to rip off his jeans with her teeth and take him in her mouth.

"I would be lying if I said I didn't. Did you think about me?" She braced herself for the truth.

"I wondered what happened to the little girl I once knew. I asked Katy about you, but as you know, she's always very vague when it comes to giving answers." His pupils dilated as he looked slowly down her body. "But you can bet your ass if

I had known you'd turned into such a beauty, I would have moved heaven and earth to track you down."

She could smell his arousal and felt her own lust dampen her panties. A surge of disappointment zipped through her when she remembered he couldn't smell her. If he could, would he still want her? Or was he just attracted to the visual?

He clamped a large hand around her waist and tugged her close. Her breasts pushed against his chest, and the heat from his body made her sink farther into his massive chest. The prickly hairs poked through her thin shirt and teased her nipples with each heavy breath.

His hand trailed up her back and cupped the base of her neck. He leaned down, angling his head for a kiss.

"Skylar." The tiny voice was like cold water being dumped on her oversexed body.

She cleared her throat and stepped away from Zane as Sophia walked into the kitchen and rubbed her eyes.

"Hey, sweetie. How'd you sleep?" She knelt down in front of the child and brushed her tangled hair away from her forehead. With dark hair that matched her eyes, she looked like a doll.

Her cautious eyes went from Skylar to Zane before landing on her again.

"This is my friend, Zane." She looked up at Zane, hoping he wouldn't intimidate the girl with his size. In the dark he was big, but in the bright light of day, he was a giant to a little girl.

"Hi." He squatted in front of the little girl and rested his elbows on his knees. "I think you might have mistaken me for a giant stuffed animal last night."

Skylar scowled and slugged him playfully in the arm. He laughed and held out his hand to Sophia.

The little one looked at his large hand and looked back at Skylar.

"It's okay. He's my friend. He may be big, but he's really nice."

She carefully placed her hand in the middle of Zane's larger one. An image of him cradling a baby to his chest flashed through Skylar's mind.

Did he want kids? Had he ever thought about settling down and mating? Was that something he wanted? Or was his job his priority and the only thing he wanted out of life?

"What's wrong?" Zane's voice shook her out of her daydreams. "You look like you just saw one of those sappy beer commercials with the horse and dog." He scowled at her.

"Nothing's wrong." She steeled her expression and smiled at the little girl. "Are you hungry, Sophia?"

"Where's the doggie?"

"The doggie left this morning," Skylar answered quickly. She decided that distraction was the best course of action. "Are you hungry?"

"I want pancakes."

"I don't have pancakes. But I do have eggs and bacon. How does that sound?" Skylar smiled.

"I want pancakes." Her bottom lip quivered.

Skylar held her breath. "Maybe we could go out and get some...?"

"How about you help me make breakfast while Skylar gets a shower?" Zane cocked his head at the little girl.

"Zane, I don't know." Sophia didn't normally do well around strangers. She was such a shy and introverted child who loved playing with her invisible playmates. Skylar had worried for the little girl ever since her mom had gotten pregnant with this last baby. What if she didn't feel special anymore?

"You know that princesses eat eggs and bacon for breakfast every day, right?" Zane gave his full attention to the little girl.

The little girl's eyes widened for a second. And just like that, her bottom lip stopped quivering. Instead of a frown, there was now a smile on her little bow-shaped mouth.

"Princesses know that eating eggs and bacon for breakfast helps the farmers make money. Every time you eat one of the things they raise or grow, it puts money in their pockets. Now if you had pancakes, well, that doesn't necessarily help anyone but the company that sells the pancake mix. So basically you're doing your job as a good princesses to help others." Zane stood to his full height.

"I want eggs and bacon." A bright smile filled her face.

Skylar's mouth dropped open. Zane's hand was at her back, guiding her into the bathroom.

"Now go get cleaned up and we should have breakfast on the table for you when you get out."

He closed the door. She blinked at the closed door for a few seconds before shaking her head.

For someone so distant and in control, Zane was unbelievably tender with Sophia.

She'd thought she had him figured out, but now she wasn't so sure. She'd just have to wait and see.

CHAPTER 43

Zane kept his eyes on the child as she leaned closer to him from her perch on the stool. He'd pulled up the tall kitchen stool near the stove so she could help lay the bacon strips in the frying pan. Once the grease started sputtering, he'd covered the pan and pulled her stool to a safe distance so she wouldn't get a grease burn.

"Easy. Not too close. Remember what I said about the cooking bacon?" He kept his voice soft so as not to frighten the child.

He remembered the frightened little girl climbing on top of his chest last night as the thunder boomed across the sky. He'd tried to explain that she needed to go back to bed with Skylar, but she was too sleepy and had conked out once her head hit his chest. With no other option, he'd resigned himself to being a human sleeping bag. It reminded him of the times Katy had come into his room when they were kids. She'd been frightened by a storm and had sought him out for protection.

Growing up as the child of Jonathan Steele, both Zane and Katy knew that once the lights were out in their parents' room, they better not disturb them. So whenever Katy got scared, she sought out her big brother instead.

He would always pretend that she was bothering him. But in reality, he was grateful for the time spent together.

"Is it ready yet?" Sophia looked up at him with brown eyes as big as saucers.

"Not yet. We need to wait until it gets crispy on both sides." He lifted the cover and turned the strips over with a fork. The meat sizzled in the pan, and the aroma made his stomach growl.

"Your tummy sounds like a dragon." She patted her small hand on his stomach.

He barked out a laugh. "I've been called a lot of things, but a dragon is not one of them."

He pulled out a white plate from the cabinet and sat it on the corner in front of her. He pulled some sheets of paper towels off the roll and handed them to her.

"I need you to put these on the plate for the bacon."

She took them out of his hand and gave the plate a thoughtful look. "Why?"

"So the grease can drain off the bacon and soak into the paper towels." He glanced at the bacon one more time.

"The bacon needs a diaper?" She looked up at him with a slight frown.

He didn't fight the grin. "I've never heard it compared to that, but, yes. Like a diaper."

Sophia wasted no time and lined up several pieces of paper on the plate.

"Perfect. Just in time, kid." He lifted the lid off the skillet and picked up the bacon with his fork. He lined the bacon strips side by side and then turned his attention back to the empty skillet. Using his fork, he whipped the eggs one last time before pouring the liquid into the hot skillet. The eggs bubbled and popped in the hot grease as they cooked.

"I hope you like scrambled."

She nodded and bent over the plate of bacon.

"How's it going? Need a hand?" Skylar came out of the bedroom in jeans, a white T-shirt, and wet hair.

His chest ached with want. She was fucking gorgeous.

"We've got it." He cleared his throat. Grabbing a spatula, he cut the eggs into pieces and turned them over to finish cooking. After a few seconds, he reached for a bowl and dumped the scrambled eggs inside.

"Sophia, what are you doing?" Skylar came up behind the girl and gave her a hug.

"Helping. It's what princesses do."

"What's going on with the bacon?" Skylar asked.

"You don't like crispy bacon?" Zane scowled. He couldn't remember how Skylar had liked her bacon when she was little.

"That's not what I meant. I meant, why does the bacon look all bundled up like a baby?" She looked up and met his gaze. A confused smile lingered on her face.

"What?" He looked over Sophia's shoulder at the plate of bacon. He chuckled. Each piece of bacon was wrapped in its own paper towel.

"Well, I did tell her the bacon needed a diaper." He shook his head. "I didn't think she was so literal."

"She's four. To her, everything is literal." Skylar grinned as she planted a kiss on the crown of the little girl's head.

"Diaper or no, let's eat. I'm starving." He lifted Sophia off the stool. "How about you, princess? Are you hungry?"

She nodded and ran over to the kitchen island and crawled up on the stool.

*S*kylar couldn't stop looking at Zane throughout breakfast. He'd been so gentle and sweet to Sophia. She didn't remember him being so thoughtful when they were kids. But then again, he'd probably thought of her as his sister's annoying friend.

As soon as they had finished their meal, she left Sophia at the island while she walked over to the stove. She set up a coloring book and crayons for Sophia to color while she cleaned up the kitchen and Zane took a shower. She was glad she'd remembered to get several changes of clothes for him. The way he kept shifting was going to have her at the store every day, buying him more clothes.

She froze with her hands in the dishwater and glanced down at Sophia.

What if he shifted in front of Sophia?

Or worse, what if he tried to harm her?

Sophia stopped coloring and looked up at Skylar.

Skylar forced a smile and kept washing the plate.

"Did you get enough to eat?"

Sophia nodded and continued coloring the chicken a shade of blue.

"I guess you're excited about seeing your grandmother today?"

She nodded but focused her attention on staying in the lines.

Skylar would never know what having a grandmother was like. Her father had never mentioned any living grandparents. The few times she'd asked if she had a grandmother, her abusive father had flown into a rage and whipped her with a belt.

She'd been no bigger than Sophia at the time.

That was her first lesson in what her childhood was going to look like.

She patted her hands on the dishtowel and took the little girl by the hand. "Let's get you changed out of your pajamas and ready to see your grandmother."

CHAPTER 46

"*W*hat's up, assholes?" Damon strode into the diner and nodded at Jaxon and Lucien before easing his big frame into the booth.

Lucien's stomach clenched as his fellow Guardian sat down across from him. He'd figured Barrett was going to send someone to check up on them. He just didn't figure it would be Damon. The brother didn't like to stay away from his mate, Ava. Lucien couldn't blame him. Ava Trahan was gorgeous.

"Damon, what are you doing here?" Lucien frowned and pushed his coffee cup away.

"Just seeing what's going on in this neck of the woods." Damon flagged down a passing waitress and ordered a coffee.

Lucien could feel Jaxon's eyes on him, but he didn't dare look at him. He knew Damon was here to find Zane.

"Where's Zane?" Damon crossed his arms over his chest and glared. "And don't fucking say you don't know." "Shit." Jaxon breathed out a heavy sigh.

Damon leaned forward and narrowed his gaze on both of

them. "Do you two understand what the penalty is for keeping information from your Pack Master?"

"I'm guessing it's not good." Lucien shook his head and locked eyes with his fellow Guardian. "Look, man, you're asking us to rat out our brother, who we've pledged to be loyal to."

"I'm asking you to be loyal to your Pack." Damon growled low and deep. The patrons sitting behind them quickly got up from their booth and headed for the door.

Lucien's heart dropped to his stomach. He was in a no-win situation. He was either going to keep Zane's situation to himself and be disloyal to his Pack, or he was going to rat out his brother.

"What if it were Jayden? What would you do?" Jaxon ran his hand through his hair.

"I would do the right thing. That's what I'd fucking do," Damon countered.

"But what if both things are the right thing to do?" Lucien insisted. "What if no matter what we do, someone is going to get hurt?"

Damon settled back into the booth and looked between them with an assessing gaze. The scar on his cheek seemed to twitch under the café lighting.

"I'm not alone." Damon cocked his head.

"Fuck." Lucien held his breath. "So Barrett is with you." Perfect. Fucking perfect. There was no way out of this shit storm now. Zane was lost, and now both he and Jaxon faced losing their jobs as Guardians because they'd been looking out for their brother.

"Not Barrett."

"Damon, there you are." Ava made her way over to their booth. "I thought you said we were eating next door at that restaurant?" She frowned and glanced over at his companions.

"Jaxon, Lucien. I didn't know you guys were in Jonesboro." She smiled.

"Hey, Ava," they answered in unison.

"They had to bring some Guardians over here to get their tatts." Damon kept his glare on them. "They decided to stay a little while longer."

"Oh yeah?" She let Damon pull her down to his knee to sit. "Is there anything fun to do here? I heard there's a club over on the other side of town."

"I wouldn't recommend it." Lucien sniffed his leather jacket and winced. "It's mainly college chicks who don't take no for an answer. Plus, it's smoky."

"I'll have to remember that." She gave Damon a warning glare.

Damon chuckled and wrapped a hand around her waist. "You don't have to worry about me."

"I wasn't. I was worried about some random bitch putting her hands on you, and then me having to put my hands on her.

Preferably around her neck." Ava gave him a pretty smile.

"So what are you doing here, Ava?" Lucien asked.

"I'm here to check on the renovation of my home."

"That's right. I forgot you had a house here." He remembered when her home had been bombed after she'd been kidnapped by red wolves. "I didn't know there was anything left."

"It was bombed pretty badly, but a good portion of the house was still standing." She shrugged. "After doing some research, I found out that it would be a good investment to have it reconstructed and put it on the market. It's not like I have any plans to move back here, not now." She glanced at Damon and grinned.

"That's smart. I hope you found a good contractor. You know they are notorious for sticking it to you." Lucien took a sip of his coffee and relaxed a little. This was good. If Ava was in the dark about why Damon was really here, then maybe they still had time to find and help Zane before Barrett found out.

He just needed a little more time.

And a whole lot of luck.

"What do you mean, you can't take her? You know I have to be on the construction site today. Especially since you're not going to be there and I missed yesterday." Skylar had too many distractions going, and she couldn't keep putting off her responsibilities. She needed to finish the house, get paid, and buy the apartment building before it got sold out from under her.

That had been the plan all along, and she wasn't about to change it for anything or anybody.

"I can't, Skylar. I can't leave Maria yet. The delivery was complicated, and the doctors said I needed to be around." His eyes grew wide with concern and the bags under them suggested he had not slept all night.

"Complicated? What do you mean?" Her stomach dropped.

Hector cradled his daughter to his chest and rubbed tiny circles on her back. She'd been happy to see her daddy when they'd arrived at the hospital and had run to him in the hallway.

"There was a lot of bleeding with the delivery. The

bleeding has stopped for now, but they are keeping an eye on it. They ended up giving her a blood transfusion."

"Oh, Hector. I had no idea. Why didn't you tell me?" She was a horrible person. She was worried about a job while he was worried about his wife's life.

"You've done so much for me already. I really hate to bother you, Skylar."

"We're friends. You can ask me for anything. You know that, right?" He'd stuck with her through thick and thin, sometimes even turning down another job that paid more so he could work with her. She'd never forget that.

"Then I need to ask you to watch Sophia another day." He cringed as he said the words.

"Where's Grandma?"

"Grandma had some car trouble. She's getting it fixed today and hopefully will be here by tonight or tomorrow at the latest." He shook his head.

She held out her hands. Sophia went willingly into her arms and stuck her finger in her mouth. "We'll be okay, won't we, Sophia?" The little girl nodded.

"Skylar, are you sure? I mean, I can get the neighbor to give her some Benadryl and watch her."

"Are you crazy? You know she'll get hives, maybe even a stronger allergic reaction, if she goes over there. I can take her." She met Sophia's big brown eyes. "You don't mind spending another night with me, do you?"

"I like it at your house. You have a doggie."

Hector barked out a laugh. "A doggie? I had no idea you had a dog."

"Not all the time. He just comes around when he's hungry." She smiled at her inside joke.

"Thanks, Skylar. I really appreciate it." He frowned. "What are you going to do about work today?"

"Don't worry about it. Just stay here and concentrate on getting your wife better." She smiled. "How's the baby?"

A grin crossed his face. "She's beautiful. Just like her mother."

"Ah, another girl. I hope she gives you a hard time." She laughed.

"I'm sure she will. We named her Sky."

CHAPTER 48

Skylar held Sophia's hand as they walked out of the hospital. She was immediately greeted with a hot blast of stifling heat the second she stepped outside. She squinted against the bright sun as she headed toward the truck.

She was still in shock that they thought enough of her to name the baby Sky. They were not related by blood, but they'd forged a friendship through the trials of life, and sometimes those bonds were just as strong.

She brushed a tear away from her cheek as she opened the door to her truck.

"What's wrong?" Zane frowned.

"Nothing."

"It's not nothing. You're crying. What's wrong?"

"They named the baby Sky."

"After you. She must be beautiful." His eyes softened.

She froze, mesmerized by the sincerity in his face. Shifting her weight, she looked away.

"Why do you do that?"

"Do what?" she asked as she gathered the child into her

truck and buckled her in the car seat. She'd bought the seat at a garage sale and kept it on hand in case she needed it for Hector's kids.

"Why do you look so uncomfortable when I give you a compliment? You must know how beautiful you are." He reached for her hand. His fingertips grazed the back of her arm and sent shivers up and down her spine.

Lying had never really been Skylar's forte. It was what had gotten her in trouble as a little girl, and she didn't see any reason to start lying now that she was a woman.

"I have red hair. I'm not a blonde or a brunette. I have qualities that men don't consider beautiful. So when you say those things, it makes me uncomfortable, because I know they're not true."

His gaze narrowed, and the air between them thickened until it was hard to draw an easy breath.

Wordlessly, he stalked around the truck, moving with slow deliberation until he stood inches from her.

"Hear me when I say this. I don't lie. I never have." His ice blue eyes flashed with anger, and his chest heaved with each carefully chosen word. "Whoever fed you the bullshit that you are not beautiful is, and will always be, a liar. Jealousy often makes people say untrue things. Your qualities that you so eloquently speak of are unique. Hair as fiery as the sun itself and eyes the color of rare gems are qualities that not every woman possesses. But they are qualities that every woman desires. And you are every man's fantasy. When I look at you, you make me lose any control that I ever thought I had. Here, standing next to you, it's all I can do not to pull your jeans down and take you up against the truck."

Her mouth dropped open.

Her body tingled in all the right places. She leaned into him.

CHAPTER 49

"Don't start something you cannot finish, Zane." She wanted to tease him to the point of no return. She wanted him wild and out of control.

"Skylar," he growled, yet he didn't move away. He held his ground as his gaze dipped to her parted mouth.

"Skylar, I'm thirsty," Sophia called out from inside the truck.

She resisted a groan and stepped back. "Okay, sweetie, we'll stop and get you a drink."

"What's up with little bit? I thought you were dropping her off with her father."

"Change of plans. It seems Grandma isn't here yet. So I'm letting her stay a little while longer." She slid into the truck and gave the little girl a smile before glancing back at Zane. "So after we stop at the gas station and grab something to drink, I'll drive you over to get your bike, and then I'll head out to the work site."

She had a four-year-old in tow, a werewolf who couldn't control his shift staying at her apartment, and she was behind schedule with work on her house.

She sighed and threw the truck into gear and pulled out of the parking lot.

So much for things going according to plan

CHAPTER 50

*Z*ane watched as Skylar drove away from the tattoo shop. He didn't let his eyes leave her until she was out of sight. Then he turned his attention to his bike.

Matt was a man of his word. He'd kept Zane's Harley locked up in the parking area behind the Moon Goddess Tattoo Shop. After finding out from Matt that both Lucien and Jaxon were still in town looking for him, he knew he didn't have time to waste. Now that he had his bike, he needed to get a solid lead on whoever was dealing meth in Jonesboro. He had a hunch that would lead him to the were-wolf who'd escaped the drug bust that night.

He grabbed the tarp draped over his bike and snatched it off.

A smile stretched across his face as he caressed his bike with his gaze.

"Hey, baby. I missed you." He ran his hand gently down the blood-red Harley Davidson Breakout. Bright red and chrome, she was dressed out like one badass bitch. Some of the other Guardians, like Damon and Jayden, had chosen colors like black and gray for their Breakouts, but not him.

He'd always been partial to red. He associated the color with courage and fearlessness.

He grinned as Skylar's face popped into his mind. Apparently he liked his women like he liked his Harleys. Hot, red and full of fire.

He straddled his bike and started the engine. The motor rumbled to life, growling between his legs.

His blood heated as he revved the engine. He loved this. The sound of his Screaming Eagle pipes, the smell of leather and metal, and the feeling of freedom and power. This was his office, astride a Harley.

He gunned the engine and pulled out onto the street. He didn't miss the stares the women on the sidewalk were shooting at him as he cruised down the street. Humans always wanted a biker. What they didn't know was that with him, they were getting a werewolf biker.

He made a right at the corner and kept his speed under the limit until the streets became a highway. He pointed his bike in the direction of Skylar's construction project and sped down the highway, letting the wind and the sun seep into his soul.

"I'm hungry." Sophia looked up at Skylar from under the hard hat she'd made the little girl wear. A bead of sweat trickled from her temple down her plump cheek. She swiped the back of her dirty hands across her face, leaving behind a smudge of brown.

The little girl had played happily under the tree in the backyard, pushing discarded pieces of wood blocks around in the dirt like cars while Skylar oversaw the continued work on the kitchen.

"I'll grab our lunch out of the truck and we'll eat, okay?" She jogged over to her truck and opened the door. Thank goodness she'd stopped at the store for some sandwich fixings, snacks, drinks, and a cooler before heading back to the construction site. So far, she'd given Sophia two snacks of animal crackers and it wasn't even noon yet.

Tugging the cooler and the bag out of the truck, she headed back toward the tree.

She found a grassy spot and sat down before pulling out the antibacterial gel. Bathing her hands, she held out the bottle to Sophia, who held out her palms. She squirted a generous amount into her hands and instructed her to rub them together. She pulled out some paper towels and wiped the excess off the little girl's hands.

After making the first ham and cheese sandwich, she handed it to Sophia. Opening a bag of chips, she placed it between them and then snagged two ice-cold waters out of the cooler.

She quickly made herself a sandwich as she watched Sophia eat in silence. The little girl pulled off the brown edges of the bread before taking her first bite.

Skylar smiled. She knew better than to give a four-year-old a sandwich with crust. She'd seen too many families out at the park having a picnic, and not once did the children have a sandwich with crust on it.

She took a bite of her sandwich and wondered if maybe she should take Sophia to the park once she finished the project.

It was hard to know how to treat a child well when she'd never been shown an ounce of kindness by her own father when she was growing up.

Her mind drifted back to Zane.

His family had been the only ones to ever treat her like she was worth something. If it hadn't been for them, who knew what would have happened to her? She might have ended up on drugs or homeless or even dead.

Girls like her needed a safe place where they could escape from abusive families the system couldn't keep track of. She was bound and determined to make her life count for something. That was her mission. To build a safe haven.

Sophia picked up a chip and nibbled on it like a little bunny.

"Hey, Skylar, you need to come look at this," Sanchez, one of her construction workers, called out from the kitchen door.

"Be right there." She brushed the hair out of Sophia's face and then hopped to her feet.

She jogged over to the back of the house where Sanchez was waiting for her. The young man was only a few years older than her but was married with two kids. He was a Were and had mated his high school sweetheart right out of school and had never gone to college. He said he never was one for studying, so he went into construction work. He was a hard worker and smart too.

She had told him he would be running his own construction company in a few years.

"What's up?" She walked into the kitchen and looked at Sanchez.

"The cabinets are the wrong color." He waved his hand at the kitchen counters sitting on the middle of the floor.

"What? That's impossible." Her heart dropped.

"We ordered maple cabinets, but these are cream-colored with a glaze."

"This can't be." Her chest tightened as she stared at the cabinets. "Even if we got the correct cabinets by the end of the week, we still won't make our deadline."

"What do you want to do?" Sanchez rested his hands on his hips, awaiting her next order. That's how Sanchez always was. So damn even-keeled.

Sucking in a deep breath, she bent down to pull the protective covering away from the cabinet. The cabinets were glazed in an off-white cream. They were a completely different look from the style the owner had picked out. She cocked her head. She liked them even better than the ones that the owner had picked out.

"Does the supplier know they sent the wrong cabinets?"

"Not yet." Sanchez arched his eyebrow. "They will."

She stood up and glanced over at the sample of the granite countertop sitting atop the work table.

She picked up the sample and held up next to the cabinet. The cabinets brought out the cream and gray colors of the granite and made it pop.

She reached in her jeans pocket, pulled out her phone, and snapped a few photos.

"To be honest, I think they look better with this countertop." She scrolled through her contacts.

"So what do you want us to do?" Sanchez asked. By this time, the rest of the workers had filtered into the kitchen. They stood there, casting worried glances at each other.

"I want everyone to grab a quick lunch, and then I want you to put these cabinets in."

"But they're not the ones the owner wanted," Sanchez said.

"I'm about to change the owner's mind." Skylar pulled up the number for the distributor. "But first, I'm calling the distributor to let him know he's giving me these cabinets for the same amount as the first cabinets. It was his mistake after all."

"What's wrong?" Damon could see the distress on Ava's face as soon as she got off the phone.

"The cabinets came in, but they are the wrong ones." Her phone dinged, and she glanced down at it.

"Then the contractor needs to fix the mistake." He shook his head. "I knew this was a bad idea, hiring someone without meeting them in person. You can't do a remodel without being there for all the damn details."

"She sent me a picture." Ava nibbled on her bottom lip. "She says the new cabinets are more expensive."

"I'm not paying one more cent." He crossed his arms.

"Well, she said that since it was a mistake, they would let us have them for the same cost as the original cabinets." She held up the phone. "Look at the picture. I think these cabinets actually look a lot better. What do you think?"

He took the phone and studied the picture.

"Still, they made a mistake. I don't want someone you are doing business with taking advantage of you." He handed her the phone back.

She grinned. "So you like them. I knew it."

"When are we driving out there?" He needed to lay eyes on this contractor.

"Now, if you're free from whatever top-secret business Barrett has you on?" She gave him a saccharine smile.

"Smartass."

"You like my smart ass," she quipped.

"You're right. I do love your ass." He reached out and clamped two hands on her butt and pulled her into his arms.

She giggled as she snuggled into his chest.

"So let's go right now." She wrapped her arms around his neck and pulled him down for a kiss.

He covered her mouth with his, taking his time to savor her sweet taste. He loved her with an intensity that frightened him at times.

"Fine. Let's go." He gave her ass a squeeze.

His phone buzzed in his jeans pocket.

"Ugh. Ignore it." She narrowed her eyes.

"Can't, babe. Might be work." Reluctantly, he pulled away from her and reached in his back pocket for his phone. He sighed as soon as he saw it was Barrett calling.

"Ignore it." She tried rubbing her boobs against his chest in an attempt to distract him.

"It's Barrett. I have to answer it." She frowned as he hit the green button.

"Hey."

"What the fuck took you so long? I was beginning to think you'd run off with those other three assholes who can't manage to answer their fucking cell phones," Barrett rumbled.

Damon fought a smile. His Pack Master was known for keeping his cool, but these last few days had certainly pissed off Barrett to put him on edge like this.

"I've got Ava here distracting me. Not planning on

running off with anyone else." He winked. "No visuals. Please." Damon laughed.

"What have you found out? Where are my Guardians?"

Damon took a deep breath. "I tracked Lucien and Jaxon to a café this morning, where they looked like they were either hung over or their dog died."

"That dog better not be Zane." Barrett growled.

Damon shook his head. "Look, boss, I'm not sure what's going on with those two, but I do know they are hiding something."

"Has Zane gone rogue?" Barrett's voice was eerily calm. Damon knew his Pack Master held Zane in the highest regard. He was his second-in-command.

"I'm not sure," Damon answered as honestly as he could. "But that's what I'm here to fucking find out."

*L*ucien ran his hand through his hair and clenched his jaw.

"Dude, you look constipated." Jaxon walked past him in the littered yard of an abandoned apartment complex and stopped at the entrance. They'd gotten a tip from a female attendant at the local gas station that this was where you could score some meth. "Fuck off, Jaxon." Lucien scowled and then glanced around at his surroundings. The apartment building was situated in an industrial part of town near the railroad tracks. The windows had been boarded up with plywood that was decorated with graffiti. The dark, dreary brick had a thick green blanket of ivy crawling up the side. The yard was bare without any grass. Not even weeds wanted to put down roots in this depressing place.

"The door is padlocked." Lucien lifted his head. His gaze landed on the roof, where a good portion of the tiles had been blown off.

"Let me run around back and see if there's another way in." Jaxon jogged around the back of the abandoned apartment.

The Arkansas sun beat down on Lucien with a vengeance. Sweat beaded at his temple, and he swiped at the moisture with the back of his hand. Probably not the best idea to wear his leather jacket today.

Lucien clenched his fists. He felt like he was letting Zane down. He seemed to have disappeared into thin air, and no one had a bead on him.

He had to hurry up and find him before Damon did.

"I got something back here," Jaxon called out.

Lucien made his way around the back of the building. His gaze landed on something poking out of the ivy. He stopped, bent down, and brushed the vine out of the way.

Concealed in the greenery was small plastic sandwich bag. He picked it up and held it up to his nose. Though it was empty, the scent of crystal meth was overpowering to his wolf's sensitive nose.

"So we have found a trail after all." Clutching the bag, he made his way over to Jaxon.

Jaxon frowned as he shoved the bag under his nose.

"Jesus, dude. That shit stinks." Jaxon stepped back.

"At least we are following the right breadcrumbs. Or should I say 'meth crumbs'?" He tossed the bag on the ground. "What did you find?"

"We have a basement window." He pointed to the boarded-up window that was too small for anyone, let alone a werewolf, to fit through.

"Are you kidding? I don't think a six-year-old could fit through there."

"Wait. I'm not finished." Jaxon walked over to the window and grabbed the board on the window. A click sounded, and then the board, along with a sizeable section of the brick, swung open. It was about a four-by-three-foot opening.

"What the fuck?" Lucien's mouth dropped.

"I know, right? I mean, how genius is it to put a concealed

door at the smallest window in the whole building? No one would have ever thought to try to get in here." Jaxon smirked and pulled out his cell phone. He opened the flashlight app and shone it into the dark basement.

"Which means these are some highly motivated drug dealers." Lucien pulled out his phone and snapped a photo of the hidden door. His Pack Master would be very interested in seeing this.

Lucien stepped inside the basement and Jaxon followed after him.

The scent of years of filth and dirt mixed with mildew had him wrinkling his nose up in disgust. The faint scent of crystal meth and sex lingered in the air in a far corner of the room.

"Yep. Drug house for sure. I'm surprised the scent isn't overwhelming." Jaxon held up the phone to a far corner of the room. Old blankets and empty baggies were littered across the concrete floor. All evidence that the users would get high and party.

"I think it's been a few days since they last used in here." Lucien held up his own flashlight app and scanned the room. Other than garbage, there wasn't much in the room.

"Let's go see what's up there." Lucien nodded toward the stairs that led to the first floor.

Jaxon followed his lead.

The door at the top of the stairs was locked. Lucien rammed his shoulder into the wood and the door gave and swung open.

He stepped into the darkened hallway of the building and blinked, allowing his eyes to adjust to the darkened room. Tiny slivers of light filtered in through the cracks of the boarded-up windows.

Wordlessly, they wandered through the litter-filled hallways, stopping only to peek into the rooms they passed.

There were old, moldy mattresses in some of the rooms, suggesting that maybe it had once been a den of homeless people until the drug dealers had taken over for their own gain.

The scent of old urine wafted around Lucien, and he swallowed back the bile rising in the back of his throat.

"Why can't people walk a few feet to go outside and take a piss instead of pissing inside?" Jaxon growled.

"Because they don't give a fuck, I suppose." Lucien wrinkled his nose and continued the trek. When he reached the last room, he nodded toward the stairs.

"Want to see what's on the next two floors?" Lucien wiped his sweaty forehead with the back of his arm.

"Why not? But I suspect it's just going to be more of the same.

More stink. More piss," Jaxon hissed.

"Probably." Lucien snorted.

A few minutes later, after making the trek to the second floor and not finding anything out of place, they forced their way up to the third and last floor of the apartment building.

They turned left at the top of the stairs and opened the door to the first room.

What Lucien saw made the hair on his neck stand at attention.

"Jaxon, check this shit out." He pushed the door all the way open and stepped inside. Jaxon was right behind him, muttering a curse.

This window was different. Instead of being boarded up from the outside, it was boarded from the inside. On either side of the window were two automatic assault rifles propped against the peeling wallpaper, and in the corner was a crate of ammo.

"What the hell have we stumbled upon?" Jaxon's gaze

darted around the room. "Why would someone leave thousands of dollars of guns and ammo in this shit hole?"

"My guess is because they are coming back." Lucien jogged out into the hallway. "Check all the rooms."

"For what?"

He met his brother's gaze. "I'm betting that each corner room with a window has the exact same setup. It's like a guard post. Go check that end and I'll get this end."

Lucien went to room opposite and opened the door. He wasn't surprised to see another window boarded up from the inside with guns resting against the wall. He ventured farther into the room and over to the window. He felt around the edges of the wood panel covering the window until his fingers brushed against a hook and latch. Flicking the hook up, he pulled on the wood. The wood panel swung open from a side hinge that had been screwed into the wall, allowing the whole board to swing free.

Sunlight filtered into the darkened room, and he rested his hands on the top of the windowsill and gazed out. His position offered an unobstructed view of the back of the building and of the backyard.

Heavy footsteps echoed down the hall with Jaxon's approach.

"Hey, you're right. Both rooms on the end are set up the same. I noticed a latch on the side of the window in both rooms and both windows open up." Jaxon rested his hands on his hips.

"This isn't just some low-rent drug-dealer setup." Lucien's gaze rested on the guns. "This is something else. And my gut tells me that it's going to help lead us right to Zane."

"*W*hat the hell is she doing?" Zane mumbled to himself as he pulled into the driveway of the construction site. His gaze zeroed in on Skylar with her hands full of a large kitchen cabinet. It was obvious she was struggling to get it from the back of a truck into the house.

He stopped his Harley by her truck and killed the engine. Setting the kickstand, he slid off the bike and jogged over to her.

"Here, let me." He took the large cabinet out of her hands, despite her protests.

"It's not that heavy. I can carry it." She pouted as he ignored her.

"Doesn't matter. You shouldn't be carrying it anyway. Not with all these assholes here to help." He said it loud enough so a passing worker heard him and dipped his head in embarrassment.

"They offered, but I told them I could do it."

"Figures," he mumbled as he stepped into the kitchen. "Where do you want this?" He turned to face her.

"Over there. It's the last cabinet that needs to be hung." She motioned with her hand.

He carried it over and hefted it up to the worker standing on a ladder. He held the weight from the bottom while the cabinet was screwed into the wall.

Once it was secure, he stepped back and admired the work.

"This looks really good. Did you pick these out yourself?"

She grinned. "Not exactly. The owner picked out a different set of cabinets, and these were delivered by mistake." That couldn't be good.

"Don't look so worried. I already talked to the owner and sent a text with the new cabinets and explained what happened. I think she liked the fact that I talked the supplier into letting us have these for the same cost as the other ones." She shrugged. "In the end, it worked out."

"Wow. I got to say I'm impressed. You must be one hell of a businesswoman."

"No, I'm one hell of a construction worker."

He didn't suppress his smile as he let his gaze drift over her body.

Her T-shirt sleeves were rolled up to her shoulders, revealing her toned arms. Sweat dripped from the ponytail she was rocking onto the front of her shirt, making the fabric cling to her like a second skin. Her jeans were tucked into her work boots, and her tool belt hung off her hips at an angle.

"What?" She crossed her arms over her chest and cocked her hip.

"Never thought I would be saying a tool belt was sexy." He grinned.

Sanchez coughed and cleared his throat while Skylar's face went as red as her hair.

"We need to get busy since the owner will be coming by

today." Sanchez continued to ignore Zane and turned his attention to her.

"I know. Too much to do and not enough workers." She brushed her hair out of her eyes.

"I can help," Zane offered.

"You?" Skylar's skeptical eyes matched what he was feeling.

He'd never done construction work in his life. But now he was suddenly feeling all Bob the Builder.

"Sure. Just show me what needs to be done." He glanced at Sophia as she entered through the back door. Her hair was messy, her clothes were dusty, and she was clutching a block of wood in her chubby hand.

"Hey, little bit."

"Hey, Zane," Sophia quipped before wrapping her hand around

Skylar's thigh and resting her head. "Skylar, I'm thirsty."

"I'll get you a drink, honey." Skylar's fingertips trailed though the little girl's dark strands.

Zane's heart clutched with longing. Mesmerized, he couldn't move or tear his gaze away from the sweet interaction between Skylar and the little girl. She was a natural with the child. An image of Skylar with a baby in her arms filled his mind. With *his* baby in her arms.

Skylar looked up at Zane and narrowed her gaze. "What? Why are you looking at me like that?"

"I don't know what you're talking about." He quickly looked away and forced his mind on other things, like the job at hand, instead of imagining what Skylar would look like pregnant. "Tell me what needs to be done."

That stupid drug in his system was making him crazy with these feelings and images. Fuck, what he wouldn't give to get back to his normal self.

"Well, since all the cabinets are in, we need to get new

measurements for the countertop. These new cabinets are bigger than the ones we ordered." She glanced down at her phone. "They close in half an hour. We can't get the order to them today, but if we get the measurements done and take it to them first thing in the morning, then hopefully they can have the granite cut in a day or so."

"That fast?" Zane picked up a tape measure. She handed him the plans and a pen so he could write the measurements down.

"It helps that Jonesboro has its own granite and stone place in town. I know the owner, and he understands that I'm on deadline. So I'm hoping he will make my countertop the priority." Skylar worried her lip with her teeth.

"I'm sure you can convince him. You seem to be quite the negotiator." He stepped toward her, wanting to kiss her.

"Skylar, I'm thirsty."

"Oh, right. I'm sorry."

"Here, I'll get her something to drink if you tell me where the drinks are."

"By the tree out back in the cooler." She sighed. "Thanks."

He headed out the back door.

The heat blasted him in the face. At least in the house there were fans to stir up a slight breeze and disperse the humidity.

A plume of dust caught his eye as a car sped up the driveway. He didn't know what kind of asshole was behind the wheel, but he was sure going to have a talk with them about driving way too fast with Sophia running around...

Snatching a drink out of the cooler, he stalked back to the house.

"Skylar, someone's here. And they are driving way too fast." He unscrewed the top of the chilled water bottle and handed the bottle to Sophia. The little girl smiled before taking a long drink. Her sweaty hair had matted to her face, but she didn't look like she minded one bit. She looked like she was having the best time playing in the dirt. It reminded him of when Skylar was little and playing in their front yard.

"Oh, my gosh. It's the owner. She's here early." Skylar wiped her hands nervously on her thighs and glanced around the room as if wondering how she could magically put the kitchen back together within seconds.

He chuckled. "Relax. The owner knows it's a work in progress. She's not expecting it to be move-in ready." He tugged her into his chest.

She relaxed for a second before stepping back. "I know, but I was hoping to have much more done. I wanted it finished early."

He cupped her cheek and forced her to look into his eyes. "Breathe."

Nodding, she closed her eyes and sucked in a deep breath.

The car pulled into the yard and stopped. She stepped out of his arms and dusted off her T-shirt.

"Can you help Bart unload the wood floor from the truck? I'd like for the owner to get a glimpse so I can show her how it's going to look once it's installed."

"Sure." He pressed a kiss to her lips before heading out the back door while she went out the front to greet her customer.

"Skylar said to put these in the living room for now, since she's giving the tour to the owner in the kitchen." Bart swiped his forehead with a black bandana and let down the tailgate of the truck. "I'll be glad when we're done. This has been one hell of a job."

"How long have you guys been on this project?" Zane hefted a pile of boxes with ease while Bart grabbed only two. The man grunted as he followed Zane to the front of the house.

"A few months now. It's undergone a dramatic change since we first started."

"It seems like it."

"Dude, you don't understand." Bart chuckled as he stepped up the front steps and into the house.

"What do you mean?"

"I mean, the whole back of the house was blown out. Like a goddamn bomb." He lowered his voice and leaned into Zane. "If you ask me, I think the owner is into something dirty. Like the mafia. How else would you explain a bombing in someone's house?"

Unease skidded across his spine and up his neck. Why didn't Skylar mention that to him? He didn't really figure the mafia was interested in setting up territory in Arkansas.

He set the wood floor down as the voices of women drifted out from the kitchen. His senses immediately became alert as the familiarity of the female voice dawned on him.

He thought back to a few months ago when the Guardian compound had been bombed after a female had been kidnapped. Then they had gotten word that the female's house had been bombed as well.

Holy shit.

This wasn't just any client's house. He was standing in Ava's old house.

This meant one thing. Damon was not far behind.

CHAPTER 54

*S*kylar smiled as she walked around the kitchen and pointed out the progress to Ava Trahan and her grandmother. "As you see, the cabinets are done, and once we get the countertops in, we can start on the hardwood floors."

Skylar hadn't expected the owner to be so beautiful, or to be around her own age. When they had Skyped, Ava never could get her camera to work, so Skylar had never seen her until today.

"Are you sure you want to sell this place, Ava?" Her granny peeked out the window over where the sink would soon be. "It's so quiet and peaceful. You and Damon could make this a second home, or just keep it for when you want a girl's retreat." Granny smiled.

"I don't need a girl's retreat. I don't want to be away from Damon as it is. The only reason he's in Jonesboro with me is because he's working some top-secret drug case for Barrett." Ava clamped her mouth shut and winced as she looked at Skylar. "Probably shouldn't have said that."

"Yeah, and now we're going to have to kill the pretty

contractor to keep her quiet." Granny shoved her hand in her white purse and dug around.

Skylar laughed a little at the offhanded comment. Surely the old woman was joking. She'd never had cause to be nervous around a client before. She'd not been worried when Ava told her the house had been bombed. Hell, she had bought the story Ava gave her about some crazy kids throwing a pipe bomb in the house. She said it was a horrible Halloween prank.

"Just kidding, hon." Granny pulled out a peppermint, stuck it between her wrinkled lips, and smiled.

"Want one?" Granny held out a second piece of candy.

"Sure." She relaxed and reached for the candy.

Granny's smile faltered and she leaned in closer. Her nostrils flared. Narrowing her eyes, the old woman spoke. "If I didn't know any better, I'd say you, my dear, are a wolf."

CHAPTER 55

"*W*hat did you say?" Skylar felt the blood drain from her face as her gaze darted between the two women. She inhaled deep, and for the first time since they had entered the house, she caught their scent.

They were wolves. Gray wolves.

"How'd did I miss that?" Ava was now staring at her with interest.

"Probably because Skylar smells different. She's not a gray. She's a red wolf." Granny frowned.

"A what?" Fear flashed through Ava's widened eyes. She took a step back, bumping into the corner of a cabinet. She flinched at the pain but didn't for one second take her eyes off Skylar.

Dread, cold and suffocating, wound itself around Skylar's body. She knew what other Weres thought of red wolves and how they were looked down upon. The only time she'd forgotten that she was different from other werewolves was when she was with Zane's family. They knew what she was from the beginning and had been accepting of her. It was because of them that she wanted to show others that not all red wolves were bad.

But now, looking at these two women, she realized that she'd been wrong to hope for such a thing.

They would always see her as the enemy.

"Skylar, I'm hungry." Sophia came running into the room with her wooden car.

Skylar scooped her up in her arms and held her close. She glared at the women. If they so much as tried to touch her Sophia, Skylar wouldn't hesitate to retaliate. "Okay, sweetie. Just a few more minutes. I think these two ladies were just leaving."

"Well, hello, sweetie." Ava's nostrils flared, scenting the little girl. Frowning, she looked over at Granny before addressing Sophia. "What's your name?"

Sophia buried her face into the crook of Skylar's neck and said nothing.

"She's a little shy around new people," Skylar said. Except with Zane. Sophia hadn't been the least bit shy around him. "Her name is Sophia."

"I didn't know you had a little girl." Ava glanced at Skylar's bare ring finger. And while Weres mated for life, they didn't always have a wedding or wear wedding rings. Rings were a personal preference, not the rule.

"She's not mine. I'm watching her for a friend. His wife had a baby and he's staying at the hospital with her," Skylar blurted out in her defense.

"How nice of you. That's good he has a friend to help him out." Ava reached out and touched a dark curl on Sophia's head.

"I have a snack in my purse that she can have." Ava met Skylar's gaze. "This is, if it's okay with you."

"I don't know…" She glanced down at the little girl in her

arms. She sensed the women didn't trust her, but somehow, her gut told her they meant no harm to the little girl.

Her unease lessened. Granny might be a bit . . . odd. But Ava seemed to be a straight shooter. She liked to know where she stood with people.

"As long as it's not candy." The last time Sophia had been at her house, Skylar had given the little girl a mini candy bar before dinner. It had amped her up and she hadn't gone to sleep until after midnight. Lesson learned.

"It's a doughnut." Ava gave her a sheepish grin. "From this morning."

Sophia's head snapped up.

"It's just a glazed one. Maybe the glazed ones don't have a whole lot of sugar." Granny shrugged. "Or she can have some chocolates that I keep in my purse." The old woman patted her white bag.

"No," Ava and Skylar answered in unison.

"I want a doughnut." Sophia looked expectantly at Skylar. Her eyes were wide as she smiled.

"I guess I don't have much of a choice now, do I?" She touched her forehead to the child's.

Ava pried open her purse and fished out the treat. She unwrapped it from the decorative paper and held it to Sophia.

"Here you go, sweetie."

Sophia grabbed the doughnut in both hands and took a big bite.

"Looks like you were hungry." Ava brushed a strand of hair out of her way.

"What do you say, Sophia?" Skylar whispered.

"Thank you," she mumbled with her mouth full of the sweet treat.

"Aw, you're welcome. I love doughnuts." Ava smiled.

"Ava loves anything sweet. Good thing you have a

metabolism like a cheetah on crack. Otherwise, you'd be big as a house," Granny said

Skylar let Sophia slide out of her arms. The little girl ran outside to her tree and sat down in the shade. Skylar turned her attention back to the women.

"Look, I wasn't trying to be deceitful by not telling you I was a red wolf when you hired me. If I had known you were a Were, I would have been up-front with you." Skylar swallowed the lump in her throat and lifted her chin. "I know how it is between our races."

"Skylar, do you have any family here in Arkansas?" Granny cocked her head. The scowl was back on the old woman's face.

"The only family I had was my father. And he's dead." She shrugged. "After I was old enough to leave home, I moved out of state. By that time, the majority of the red wolves had eliminated themselves. I was hoping to move back and live a quiet life. Without any drama." Her throat ached, but she forced herself to continue.

"I will understand if you don't want me working on your house anymore. If you would agree to just pay me what I'm owed for the work done, then I'll be out of your way."

"Did you know that it was red wolves who bombed this house in the first place?"

"What?" Skylar blinked and shook her head. "There's not that many left. Why would they do such a thing?"

"Because they got upset when Ava was rescued from them. They were holding her captive. They wanted to use her to increase their population." Granny kept her steady gaze on her.

"Oh, god." Her hand clutched her stomach and she reached out to the nearest cabinet to keep herself from falling. Nausea swelled in her stomach. She knew what red wolves were capable of. She just never thought they'd be so ballsy to take a gray female.

"I'm so sorry. That's horrific."

Ava sucked in a deep breath and blew it out. "What's done is done. It's in the past. I'm here to talk about the future. Skylar, I am thrilled with the progress. I think you've done the impossible and turned this house back into a livable place." Ava shook her head. "After it was bombed, I didn't think it could ever be fixed. But you have proved me wrong." Ava smiled. "Good job."

"Thank you." Skylar was humbled by Ava's generosity and praise. After all the woman had gone through, she was still willing not to judge Skylar based on someone else's actions. "Does this mean you want me to finish the house?" "Absolutely." Ava nodded.

Skylar felt the weight lift off her shoulders. She'd needed this job, and now she had gotten validation from Ava that she was pleased. She knew she was going to be able to make her dream a reality. She was one step closer to getting her paycheck and being able to buy the apartments.

CHAPTER 56

Zane hurried out the front door and headed for his Harley. He needed to make himself scarce before Ava saw him.

Tony, one of the younger construction workers, stood off to the side, talking animatedly into his cell phone.

"Don't let him go out tonight! You know he's going to go to that drug party and get high. He's going to get himself killed." The young guy couldn't be older than twenty, but he was obviously worried about someone getting drugs.

Zane stopped in his tracks and waited until the guy hung up. The Hispanic worker scowled when he spotted Zane.

"Look, tell Skylar I've got to go. I know she's up to her ass in work here, but tell her it's important." He ran his fingers through his hair and dug his keys out of his pocket.

"Wait." Zane grabbed his elbow. "What's going on?"

"I can't tell you. I don't know who you are but I know what you are." He frowned and tried to shake loose of his hold, but Zane wasn't about to let him leave.

Ah, so this crewman was a werewolf.

"You're right, you don't know me. But if this is about drugs, you need to let me know."

"Are you a narc or something?" The guy's eyes widened and he stepped away from him. "I don't want any trouble from the Pack."

"Hell no, I'm not a narc." He growled. "Look, I know what it's like to have someone on drugs. If you know where they are selling this shit, you need to tell me so I can stop it." And if he wasn't going to spill the info, then Zane would just beat the shit out of him until he did.

"Fine. But you didn't hear this from me." He glanced back at the house, making sure no one was watching them. "There's an old abandoned apartment building on the other side of the tracks. They deal drugs out of there, but they are real careful about who they let in. In fact, the cops are real careful to steer clear of the place. A few weeks ago, a cop got to nosing around and was found dead right out in the front yard. A single gunshot wound to his head." He glanced around and leaned in. "Word on the street is these guys are not your average drug dealers. They are big time. They have to be Weres. And once you get in to party, there's no getting out. Until they let you out." He shook his head. "My younger brother thinks he's so bad, ya know, trying to show off for his friends. He said he's going to the party tonight. I told my mother she cannot let him go. That kid is going to wind up dead if he doesn't wise up." Zane listened without interrupting.

"How do you get into the party?"

"You get an invitation—that's how my brother got invited. Someone gave it to him at school. It tells you what time to show up. That's how they know if it's someone wanting drugs or someone nosing around. If you don't show up at the right time with the invitation, then you don't get in." The guy shrugged. "Or they kill you."

He nodded. A plan slowly began to formulate in his brain. He was alone, and he was going to need a plan of attack.

"Please don't tell Skylar about my brother. She has a rule about not hiring addicts or people with addicts in their families." He shook his head. "I need this job. My dad died a year ago, and it's just me and my mom and my brother. Plus, I don't want her to be mad at me." He shifted his weight.

Zane felt bad for the kid.

"I won't say anything on one condition."

"What's that?"

"I need that invitation your brother has. I need to get into that building,"

*S*kylar frowned as she heard the rumble of a motorcycle. She excused herself from her clients and went to the front door. Zane's Breakout tore down the dirt road and turned onto the main road.

"Weird. He didn't tell me he was going anywhere," she muttered to herself.

"Don't worry, honey. Men are like that." Granny patted her shoulder. "Here one day and gone the next."

Skylar turned and forced a smile she didn't feel. She didn't like that Zane had left without saying goodbye or telling her where he was going. It felt so final.

"Yes, well..." The thunder of a motorcycle had her turning back to the front yard. Her heart lurched with hope. "Oh, that must be him. He must have forgotten something." Like telling me goodbye, she thought.

"Actually, that motorcycle is coming from the opposite direction." Ava stepped up behind them and looked over their shoulders.

The three of them stayed huddled together at the front door, watching the approaching rider.

"Oh, that's Damon." The excitement in Ava's voice was unmistakable.

"Damon?" Ava asked. She squinted as the rider approached. He, too, was riding a Harley.

"My mate." Ava skirted them and ran out into the yard to meet the visitor.

No sooner had he set the kickstand on his bike than he was off and pulling her into a tight embrace. He kissed her like he hadn't seen her in years.

The guy was as big as Zane with dark hair mostly hidden under a bandana and had a scar running down his cheek. Even from this distance, there was something lethal about the guy, and it had nothing to do with his size.

Ava jumped up and wrapped her legs around his waist as they deepened the kiss.

Skylar cleared her throat and glanced away, a little embarrassed that she'd been staring too long.

"They're always like that." Granny stepped up to her side and held out a peppermint as she watched the couple. "Like cats in heat."

Skylar snorted and then bit her lip. The old lady wasn't your typical grandmother that was for sure. Granny had spunk and she spoke her mind. Skylar wondered what her grandmother had been like. If she'd lived, would she have baked cookies with Skylar or taught her how to cook? Would she have taken her on picnics or read to her?

Would she have protected her from her father?

She turned to the older lady and smiled. "Ava didn't tell me she was bringing her grandmother. I'm so glad you could come."

"Oh, well, I'm not her grandmother by blood." Granny pursed her lips and nodded. "But I'm her granny where it counts. And that's what matters, isn't it, honey?"

"I guess." She shook her head. "I never met my grandmother. Or my mother." The words sounded pathetic, even to her.

"You must have had a wonderful father raise you." Granny patted her arm.

"Actually, no. I had to raise myself. My dad was a monster." In reality, he'd been a far worse monster than any she'd encountered in her dreams.

She stepped away from the woman's sympathetic touch. She didn't want pity.

Granny's chin lifted in the air, and she stared long and hard at her.

"Then you did a wonderful job. You have found your place in this world and accomplished so much more than a lot of people. You should be extremely proud of yourself, Skylar," Granny said.

Skylar blinked as her throat tightened. She'd never really thought about it like that. She'd been far too busy trying to make her future better to revive any old ghosts of the past.

"Thank you. I appreciate that." She looked away just as Damon and Ava walked in.

"Skylar, I want you to meet Damon." Ava rested her head on the large male's chest, and it was clear to Skylar that she was sending out a message that he was taken.

"Nice to meet you." Damon stuck out his hand.

Skylar accepted it. "Pleasure to meet you. I'm glad you could come with Ava to see the progress on the house." She waved toward the kitchen. "Come on back and I'll show you what's going on."

"It looks so good, Damon . . ." Ava's voice drifted off.

Skylar stopped and turned when she realized the couple wasn't following behind her.

"What's wrong?"

Damon's nostrils flared, as he stood frozen in the living

room. His gaze swept the room as if looking for something. His chest heaved, and his breathing grew faster.

Gritting his teeth, he looked right at her and glared.

Fear crawled around in her stomach and she felt like trapped rat on a sinking ship.

He knew she was a red wolf.

"Where is he?" Damon growled.

Her fear shifted, morphed into something deeper. This had nothing to do with her being a red wolf. This was way worse. This had to do with Zane.

Nausea swamped her like a riptide. She glanced around, looking for something to defend herself with. She'd grown up with angry Weres. She knew what was coming next.

Pain.

"Skylar, look what I found." Sophia came running into the living room and made a beeline straight for her.

Her heart tightened as she picked Sophia up and held her close, not once taking her eyes off Damon.

Damon's eyes flashed and he lunged for her.

Skylar squeezed her eyes shut and angled her body so he couldn't strike Sophia.

"Don't hurt her," Skylar cried out.

"What are you talking about?" Damon growled. "She's going to hurt herself with the damn snake in her hand." He spun Skylar around and grabbed Sophia's hand.

"What?" His words didn't compute in her adrenaline-fueled brain.

Sophia whimpered as she stared up at the large man.

Skylar glanced down at Damon's grip on Sophia's hand. She was clutching a brown snake. She had squeezed its head between her fingers while its body wrapped itself around her chubby little hand.

"Oh god." Skylar's heart pounded so hard she thought it was going to leap out of her chest.

"Don't move." Damon commanded as he grabbed the snake's head. Very carefully, he began the process of unwinding the body from around Sophia's hand. Once he had the snake in his grip and away from Sophia, Skylar sucked in a breath.

"Sophia, what were you thinking?" Skylar hugged her tight. She didn't fight the tears that flowed down her face in an avalanche of emotion.

"I found it by the tree. I wanted to keep it as my pet." Her lips quivered.

Damon examined the snake in his hand. "It's just a brown snake. Not poisonous." He cut his eyes at the little girl. "But until she knows the difference, she should treat all snakes like they're deadly."

"It could have hurt you. You must promise me never to touch another snake again." Skylar looked into Sofia's eyes. "Promise me."

"I promise, Skylar." Sophia blinked rapidly, and Skylar knew she was close to tears.

"Thank you." Skylar looked at Damon.

"That almost gave me a heart attack." Ava pressed her hand to her heart.

"Here, honey. Have some chocolate." Granny, unfazed, pulled out a piece of chocolate from her white purse and handed it to Ava. The woman was a virtual Easter Bunny.

Damon walked outside with the reptile, and when he came back he didn't have anything in his hands.

"Are you going to tell me what's going on?" He looked right at Skylar and crossed his arms over his massive chest.

"I don't know what you're talking about." She swallowed and tried to keep her tone calm.

"I'm talking about Zane," he shot back.

"Zane? Guardian Zane?" Granny cocked her head.

"Yeah. I want to know why he's been here with her." He pointed his finger in her direction, and she tried not to fidget.

"Skylar, I didn't know you knew Zane." Ava's lips quirked up.

"I've known him since I was a kid," she admitted. Sophia, clearly over her scare with the snake, wiggled her body until Skylar got the message and put her down.

"Then you won't mind telling me why he was here? Especially since he's been missing from the Pack for almost a week now."

"Zane's missing?" Ava's smile was gone. "Why didn't you tell me, Damon?"

"Because it's Pack business, and you know I can't divulge that kind of information." He kept his gaze on Skylar as he spoke to his mate.

"Is Zane okay? That's not like him, to leave without telling anyone." Ava's gaze darted from him back to her. "I mean, he's Barrett's right-hand man."

"Barrett Middleton? The Pack Master?" She knew Zane was a Guardian, but had no idea he was that high up the ranks. To be privy to the goings-on of the Pack and be relied upon by Barrett Middleton was quite impressive. And important.

"You didn't know that?" Granny cocked her head.

"I…"

"He *was* Barrett's right-hand man. Right now, he's gone rogue," Damon growled.

"What? No, he hasn't." She shook her head. "Why would you think he's gone rogue?"

"Because he threw away his cell phone, gave his Guardian brothers the slip, and hasn't been heard from. It's pretty obvious." Damon narrowed his gaze.

"That doesn't mean he's gone rogue. Zane is the most honorable and responsible person I've ever met." She held up her hands.

"Apparently, he's decided going rogue was more fun than staying a Guardian." Granny pursed her lips. "I feel bad for the guy. You know the punishment for going rogue is death."

"You're wrong—you're all wrong." She held up her hands, pleading with them. She had to make them understand. Or it would cost Zane his life.

"If he's not gone rogue, then what is it?" Damon cocked his head.

She pressed her lips together and sucked in a deep breath. Zane had trusted her, and she wasn't going to betray his confidence. "I can't say."

"Then I can only assume by the evidence I've seen that he's gone rogue." A satisfied smirk settled on Damon's lips.

Anger boiled up inside her and she curled her fingers into fists.

"He's not rogue. Just because he can't control his shift does not mean he's gone rogue," she spat out. "It's not even his fault." "What?" Ava jerked her head toward her.

Skylar's stomach sunk to the floor like a thousand-pound anchor. Holy shit. What had she done?

"What are you talking about?" Damon stepped closer, his face set in stone.

She licked her lips and shook her head. She'd said too much.

"Look, you are going to make it worse on Zane if you don't say anything, Skylar," Ava pleaded. "I know you care for him. Tell

Damon so he can help."

Skylar cut her eyes to the Were. "I don't exactly trust you."

"And why is that?"

"Not you in particular. Just not too trusting with Weres in my life."

"And Zane? Does he fit that mold?" Damon asked.

"No." She shook her head. "Zane I would trust with my life."

"Then let me help him. If you don't, then Barrett is going to assume he's gone rogue and he will have to pay the price with his blood."

"He's not rogue. He's been drugged or something and now he can't control his shift." She froze as soon as the words left her mouth. She'd betrayed him.

"What?" Ava gaped.

"That's not possible." Damon shook his head and stared at her as if she were lying.

"Look, I know it sounds impossible. But it's the truth." She looked at them. "I found him hiding in the shed out back, naked. Apparently, he shifted in an alley in town and was looking for someplace to hide."

"But how can he not control his shift?" Granny shook her head. "I've never heard of such a thing."

"I don't know, but I've seen it happen. I've been in the room when it's happened. He becomes full of rage and can't stop it. It's like he turns into a different person."

"Are you sure he's been drugged? Maybe it's just his nature now." Damon cocked his head.

"I'm sure. He said it happened after he got hurt at a drug bust." She glared. "Zane is the best Were I've ever known. Don't you dare question his loyalty to his Pack or doubt his integrity."

"If he's in trouble, then why hasn't he contacted his Pack to help? We are his brothers."

"Because he's trying to find a cure on his own. He's trying to fix the problem." She held her breath, hoping he believed her.

Damon tugged his phone out of his jeans and hit some buttons before holding his device to his ear.

"It's me. You and Lucien get weaponed up. Tonight we're going to get Zane."

"*P*lease don't do this. Please don't hurt him." Skylar launched herself at him, digging her fingers into his leather jacket. He snatched his arm away and glanced down. She'd scratched his damn leather.

"Stop it. It's okay. Damon's not going to hurt Zane." Ava stepped in between them and put her hands on Skylar's shoulders in an attempt to calm her down.

Damon frowned and headed for the door. But Skylar was persistent and threw herself in the doorway, blocking him from leaving.

He growled at the redhead, hoping she would get the hint and get the fuck out of his way, but she didn't. "Move."

"No. You're going to kill Zane, and I'm not going to let that happen." She crossed her arms and planted herself at the front door.

"Fuck, can't I get one day without hysterics?" he mumbled to himself.

"Excuse me?" Ava cocked her brow.

He winced. "I wasn't talking about you, babe. You know

that." Okay, maybe he was talking about her a little, like how she went ballistic when he had to stay overnight on a mission. But he sure as fuck wasn't telling her that.

He turned back to the redhead. "Look, if what you are saying is true, then I'm not going to kill Zane. If he's truly in trouble and not violating any of the Pack Laws, then I'm sure Barrett will help."

She looked at him like she thought he was lying through his teeth.

He didn't have time for this shit. He grabbed her by the elbows and lifted her up. She screamed and thrashed as he moved her out of the way.

Gritting his teeth, he headed out the door into the yard. The sun beat down on him like a laser. He glanced at the horizon and the sun quickly dipping low in the sky. Evening couldn't come fast enough.

"Damon, wait." Ava ran after him and grabbed his arm.

"What?" He gave a long-suffering sigh.

"You're not going to hurt Zane, are you?" She frowned as she looked into his eyes.

"Ava, I need you to trust me on this. If Zane is in trouble, I'm going to do all I can to help." He pulled her into his arms. "I love you, baby, but you've got to start putting your trust in me."

"I do trust you." She batted her eyes and snuggled in closer.

"Where do you think you're going to find him?"

"I have a lead. At the hotel by the highway," he lied.

"The nice one with the cute little courtyard?" She frowned. "That doesn't look like a place where drug deals go down."

"Exactly why it's the perfect place. Apparently they have drug parties on the thirteenth floor. I'll talk to you later tonight." He kissed her hard before jumping on his Harley.

He hated to lie to his mate, but he wouldn't put her in danger for anything.

*D*arkness had fallen and the temps were dropping to a comfortable, balmy night.

"Dude, how can you and Damon wear that leather in this heat?" Jaxon whispered from his position on his stomach in the woods by the apartment building.

"I heard that," Damon whispered loudly from his position.

"It's comforting." Lucien grinned. Damon had called and updated them about what was going on with Zane and they told him about discovering the drug party at the abandoned place.

They'd quickly realized that this was the most likely place Zane would show up if he was searching for a cure. Lucien and Jaxon had met Damon here before dark and staked out their place on the side nearest the secret entrance. Jayden and Braxton arrived shortly after the others did after Barrett gave them an update. They were currently on the other side of the building, hiding in the brush.

The moon was veiled behind a cluster of clouds tonight, but Lucien could still see the rest of his Guardian team around the building.

"Can't we get closer?" Damon shifted on his stomach and held up binoculars to get a better look.

"Fuck no, man. They've got guards at every corner window with automatic rifles. One rustle of a tree leaf and they'll blow your head off," Lucien hissed.

"I've not seen movement since we got here." Damon scowled.

"Well, I put two teens on this building starting at four this afternoon, and they both said people have been trickling in since six o'clock. They probably got high, partied, and passed out." Lucien cringed as he thought about the stinky mattresses and used condoms he'd seen on the floor earlier that day.

"Settle in, boys. It's going to be a waiting game."

CHAPTER 60

Skylar jumped as a motorcycle rumbled into the parking lot. She hurried to her apartment window and glanced out into the darkness. The biker pulled up under the security lights and took his helmet off. Her heart sunk when she realized it wasn't Zane.

She stood frozen to that spot, her gaze searching for the tiniest hope that Zane was still coming back to her.

Since she'd told Damon the truth, she couldn't shake the guilt she felt for betraying Zane's trust. He would never forgive her. She knew that in her heart. But as much as she hurt right now, she'd rather have him alive and safe.

Knock, knock, knock.

She pulled herself away from the window and smiled at Sophia, who was coloring on the couch, as she headed for the door.

Opening the door, she smiled at her visitor. "Hey, Hector. Come on in." She stepped out of the way to allow him entrance.

A happy but tired smile stretched across his face. "Hey, Skylar. How's Sophia?"

Sophia came running around the corner at the sound of her father's voice.

"Hey, baby girl." Hector caught her before she could crash into him and lifted her high in the air. She giggled and wrapped her arms around his neck in a tight hug. "Were you good for Skylar?" She nodded and he looked to Skylar for confirmation.

"She was very good. She even went to work with me today. She makes a pretty good worker."

"Of course she does. She takes after her daddy, don't cha, sweetheart?" He kissed both her cheeks.

"How are Maria and the baby?" She led him into the living room, where Sophia began gathering her coloring book and crayons.

"They're doing well. They expect her to come home tomorrow."

"That's good."

"My mom just got into town, so I'm going to drop Sophia off before going back to the hospital." He grabbed the pink backpack and stuffed the coloring book and crayons inside. "How's the house coming? Are we behind?"

"It's going good, and we are behind. But the owner came by today and loves it. I think she's going to be okay with coming in a little late. She seems very understanding." Right before Ava left, she'd assured Skylar that she wanted her on the job and not a different contractor. She even said not to stress too much about the deadline.

"Wow, that's great. I've been worried." He ran his fingers through his hair.

"No need to worry. It's all going to work out." She smiled and wished she felt the same optimism about Zane.

"Ready to go, sweetheart?" Hector took Sophia's hand in his.

"What do you say to Skylar for letting you spend the night?"

"Thank you, Skylar."

She bent down and hugged the little girl tightly. Her heart suddenly felt incredibly empty. With Zane gone and now Sophia, she felt a little lost.

"You're welcome, sweetheart. Come back soon, okay?"

"Thanks, Skylar. I can't tell you how much I appreciate you," Hector said.

"That's what friends are for." She smiled as they walked to the door.

"Nah, that's what family is for." He smiled and closed the door behind him.

The apartment was quiet. Too quiet. She'd gotten used to Zane and Sophia being around and now it just seemed wrong.

She was too wired up to go to bed, so she headed into the kitchen. Opening the refrigerator, she pulled out a beer. Popping the cap off, she took a long drink.

Knock, knock, knock.

Her heart sped up as hope rose within her chest.

Zane.

She ran to the front door and threw it open. Her joy turned to confusion as she saw Hershel on the other side.

"What are you doing here?" Her mind raced. "How did you find out where I live?"

"I know a lot more about you than you think, Skylar." Hershel grinned.

"I'm not interested in talking to you." She tried to slam the door in his face, but he stuck out his boot. He shoved the door open and stepped inside her apartment.

"Not so fast. It seems me and you got some catching up to do, little girl."

She turned and sprinted for her bedroom, but he was faster and grabbed her and knocked her to the floor.

Her gaze landed on the front door.

Mrs. Nelson. If the old lady heard her scream, she would get help.

Skylar opened her mouth and screamed. Hershel drew back his fist and struck her across the cheek.

Pain exploded in her head as stars swam in front of her eyes. She cradled the side of her face.

"Keep your mouth shut, bitch," Hershel hissed and punched her in the stomach.

She cried out as sharp pain raced through her abdomen. Curled into a fetal position, she tried to catch her breath.

Movement at the door attracted her attention. Mrs. Nelson's door opened and she stepped out when she saw Skylar's door standing open. Hershel turned to see what she was looking at. Curling his fingers into his palms he stalked toward the door.

"Run, Mrs. Nelson! Go get help!" she called out. Her vision blurred as she felt herself slip into unconsciousness.

*L*ucien's body began to cramp from holding his position on the ground. It seemed like they'd been waiting forever, and no one had entered or left the building.

A rumble of a car grew closer. Damon motioned with his hand for everyone to hold their positions.

A black van rolled into the front yard and sat there for a few seconds before a male got out of the driver's seat and walked around the back of the vehicle. He opened the back and ducked inside. Seconds later he was out of the van and carrying what appeared to be a female across his shoulders.

Lucien kept his gaze on the male as he went straight to the basement window of the building and opened the secret entrance. He fought back a growl as the guy stuffed the woman through first and then crawled in after her.

"Fuck. That's Skylar," Damon growled.

"Who?" Jaxon asked.

"Zane's woman," Damon muttered.

"Zane has a woman? Since when?" Lucien cut his eyes at Damon.

"I guess since he got here. I met Skylar today, and she had his scent all over her. She's the one who told me what was up with

Zane. Did I mention she's a red wolf?"

"Holy fuck. I didn't know there were any red females left." Lucien studied the secret entrance.

"I think we are all surprised by that information," Damon growled. "I don't think she's very fond of being associated with the red wolves. I think she's tried to keep her distance from them."

"Sounds like a smart woman." Lucien cocked his head. "Well, if that's Zane's woman, then we need to bust up in there and get her the fuck out."

"Wait, someone's approaching," Damon hissed.

They all went still as the large, shadowy figure went straight up to the front door and knocked. The guy turned and by the light of the moon, Lucien could see that it was Zane.

"Fuck, it's him. We need to warn him that his woman is in there." Lucien tensed every muscle in his body to keep from running straight up to the front door.

"Stop calling her his woman. She has a name. Skylar." Damon shook his head.

"Fine. Whatever. We need to warn..."

"Shush, the door is opening," Damon warned.

The front door opened only a few inches, enough for Zane to hand a piece of paper to whoever stood on the other side.

"Where the fuck did he get an invite?" Lucien glared at Damon.

"Not sure."

A few seconds later, the door swung open all the way and Zane walked on in.

"Okay, well, he's in. And we need to get in." Lucien's

nerves were on fire with all this waiting around. He usually wasn't this impatient, but this was Zane, and he was like a brother to him.

"TAKE the invitation up to the front door and knock," Damon ordered. "As soon as you get in, take out the guard. Then let the rest of us in one by one so the guards on the top floor don't get suspicious."

"Ease out of the trees the way we came in and approach from the front," Damon added.

"Got it." Lucien stuck the invitation in his jacket pocket and backed his way out.

As soon as he was far away to avoid being seen by anyone in the house, he stood and made his way out to the street so he could approach the front door. He just hoped he wasn't going to be too late.

Skylar slowly woke up to a throbbing pain in the side of her head. She blinked and tried to adjust her vision to the dimly lit room. The scent of piss and filth made her gag, and that only accentuated the pain in her head.

"Wake up, little girl." Hershel's voice made her tense.

She remembered him hitting her and then going after Mrs. Nelson. Everything else was a blank.

"What do you want from me? What did you do with Mrs. Nelson?" She sat up and braced herself with her palms. Something furry scurried across the back of her hand. She screamed and jerked her hand off the floor.

"So many questions." Hershel chuckled. "Don't worry about Mrs. Nelson." He grinned maniacally. "You know she was actually very helpful in letting me know your schedule."

"What?"

"It seems her grandson Luther owes me a lot of money. That old lady was more than willing to help me get to you if I didn't kill Luther."

He turned on a gas lantern, and the light illuminated the space. She glanced around at the squalor and covered her mouth with her hand. Dirty old mattresses were strewn on the floor, stained with urine and other body fluids. Condom wrappers littered the floor along with beer cans and drug paraphernalia.

She was in some kind of drug house.

"As for you, well, you know what I want with you, Skylar." Hershel leaned toward the light. He smiled evilly at her with his yellowed teeth.

She sucked in rapid breaths, trying to figure out how the hell to get out. Panic rose and welled inside her chest as images of her childhood flashed through her mind.

The door burst open, and Zane came tumbling into the room. He dropped to his knees on the floor. Her heart swelled with relief when she saw him, but it was short-lived.

Two other red wolves walked in behind him carrying automatic weapons.

"Zane?"

He glanced up at her with unfocused eyes.

"What did you do to him?" Ignoring the pain in her head, she crawled over to Zane.

"Just slowing him down a bit, that's all." Hershel laughed. "Seems like our boy Zane stumbled onto our little secret, didn't ya, asshole?"

Zane growled but didn't move from his position on the floor. She reached him and cradled his head between her palms. "Zane, what did they do to you?"

"Just put a little silver in him. I can't have him going all apeshit up in here. This is a business, you know." Hershel scowled.

"You're a drug dealer, so what do you want with us?" She glared at him over her shoulder.

"I've got a surprise for you, Skylar." Hershel walked over to the door where Zane had entered and motioned to someone in the hallway.

"Hey, little red." A tall, lanky man with a pockmarked face and rotten teeth stepped into the light.

Skylar forgot to breathe. Dale Wade stepped out of his grave and into the room.

"That's not possible. You're dead." The blood drained from her face as she stared up at her dead father.

Dale chortled. He reeked of cigarette smoke and meth. She knew he never touched the drug himself, but he sure as hell cooked it.

"It's amazing what you can get away with when you put your mind to it."

"You're supposed to be dead."

"It seems I got into a bit of trouble with these Arkansas Guardians." He glared at Zane. "Ever since Middleton became Pack Master, he's been fucking up my business, always shutting down drug deals." He spit a dark stream of tobacco juice on the floor.

She cringed.

"I figured if he thought I was dead, then he'd quit snooping around. And it worked, too, until he" — he pointed at Zane —

"fucked everything up."

"That meth house he busted a few weeks ago was my biggest factory. He destroyed all my hard work and I lost a lot of fucking money by not filling those orders." He stepped closer to her. "Hershel said he ran into you in town. So I followed you. That's when I saw you two together. I knew if you were out of the picture, then the Guardian wouldn't have any reason to stay in Jonesboro. So I sent Hershel out to that house you've been working on. I told him to make it look like an accident."

Her blood ran cold. She'd always known she was a bother to her father when she was growing up, but she hadn't thought he was capable of murdering her.

"And then Zane showed up," she whispered.

"Yeah, and once again fucked everything up." He ran his hand over his balding head. "I see I have to handle things myself around here." He pulled out a gun from the back of his pants and aimed it at Zane.

"Stop!" She leapt in front of Zane, blocking her father's aim.

He threw back his head and laughed. Hershel joined in with him, along with the two guards holding the rifles.

"You are still as stupid as you ever were. I swear, girl. Do you think I won't shoot you too?" He scratched his chest and grinned as he aimed the gun at her head and pulled the hammer back.

"Wait until I'm done with her." Hershel grinned and reached for his belt. He unzipped his pants and motioned with his head toward the dirty mattress. "Get over there and take your clothes off."

*L*ucien stepped inside the abandoned apartments after the guard verified his invitation. Rap music drifted down the hall, and the stench of meth hung heavy in the air. As the armed guard closed the door, Lucien grabbed the guy by the neck and knocked his head into the wall.

The guard was human, so he didn't kill him. He grabbed the limp guard, tossed him over his shoulder, and shoved him into the nearest closet. He locked it and glanced around to make sure no one else was coming.

He needed to get the Guardians inside as fast as possible. As much as he wanted to rush upstairs and find Zane, Lucien knew he needed to follow orders and get some backup.

He opened the door and motioned.

A jagged flash of lightning streaked across the sky, followed by a bellow of thunder. A few thick raindrops fell and soaked into the ground as he waited.

Jaxon strolled up to the front door, his head down and his hands in his pockets.

"What the fuck took you so long?" Lucien growled.

"Just trying to make it believable. Addicts don't sprint to

the door. They'd get their asses shot for coming in hot." Jaxon winked before shoving past him inside.

"There are humans here," Lucien whispered. He turned his attention back to the yard, waiting for the next Guardian to walk up.

"Fucking perfect. And here I thought I was going to shift." Jaxon sighed and reached for his gun in the back of his jeans.

"Not this time. We need to take this slow and easy. No human casualties." Lucien nodded as Braxton approached and stepped inside.

"Braxton, you go with Jaxon and secure the first floor. I'll wait on Jayden and Damon before going to the second."

Braxton and Jaxon nodded and made their way through the first floor, clearing and securing each room. By the time the first floor was swept, Damon and Jayden had made it inside.

"First floor is secured. Be advised there are humans among the Weres."

"Fuck." Damon reached into his holster and brought out his Sig Sauer. "Let's go to the second floor. Zane is in here somewhere, and so is his girl, so we need to find them."

CHAPTER 64

The pain in Zane's shoulder was astounding. No sooner had he entered the building than he'd been jumped and injected with silver. Whoever was responsible was waiting for him.

He tried to wade through the fog in his brain and focus on Skylar's face. He'd been poisoned with silver and shoved in the room where she was being held. His blood was boiling with anger, and he didn't care if the two guards with the rifles were human, he wanted to shift into wolf so he could tear their throats out.

"Zane."

He could hear Skylar's voice and was vaguely aware of what was going on, but he couldn't make his body obey a fucking command. He was trapped.

By being self-disciplined before and unable to control his body now, he'd gone from one extreme to the next.

Skylar. Her father, Dale Wade. And that asshole Hershel Baker.

He'd grown up with Hershel, and they'd been enemies from the beginning. Hershel was more of a sociopath than an asshole. He'd been accused of animal mutilations in grade school and rape in high school.

He hated that motherfucker with a vengeance.

Skylar screamed as Hershel grabbed her by the hair and threw her on the dirty mattress.

Zane knew what was coming next. He had to get control of his body before Skylar got hurt.

"$\mathscr{H}$e's not on the first or second floor. That leaves the third floor. There's a shitload of guns and ammo on that floor, so we need to be careful," Lucien whispered among his Guardians.

"Weapons ready. These red wolves that have Skylar and Zane are being cowards and using humans as guards. No shifting." Damon scowled at the group.

"Got it." Jaxon said.

"Barrett is en route. So let's try to do this nice and easy and have it all wrapped up like a Christmas present before he gets here."

SKYLAR LANDED with a thud on the dirty mattress. Hershel's hand was in the front of his pants, and she knew if she didn't get her ass up and fight, he was going to rape her.

"Remember how we used to play when you were a kid, Skylar?" Hershel rubbed his hand across his bulge in his jeans.

Her heart raced. Her breathing came in short pants.

Shivers racked her body, and she didn't bother holding back the tears that streamed down her face.

Skylar froze as her mind flooded with horrendous memories of the past. She remembered Hershel coming into her bedroom after her father had passed out. She'd tried to get away, but he'd choked her until she passed out. When she woke up, he'd been on top of her.

"This time, I want you conscious. So I'm not going to choke you. I want you awake for every second I'm inside you."

*R*ed-hot rage built up inside Zane as he listened helplessly to Hershel's vile words.

She'd been abused as a child by that pervert, and her father had stood by and let it happen.

Hershel shoved his pants down, grabbed his erection, and took a step toward Skylar.

Skylar screamed.

He was no match for the silver in his body, but the silver was no match for the animal that raged inside him.

As Zane pulsed with violent anger, his vision went white. He knew his eyes were shifting, changing to the color of bloodlust.

Throwing his head back, he growled, shattering every window in the room.

Hershel stopped and spun around, his eyes wide with surprise. Dale reached for his gun and aimed it at Zane while the two armed guards aimed their rifles at him.

"Shoot that fucker," Hershel yelled.

He didn't care if he lived or not, but he sure as hell wasn't going to let anyone hurt Skylar. Not ever again.

He'd continuously grappled for control since he'd been infected with the drug. He'd struggled with containing his shift and caging the monster inside his body. He'd fought against it for too fucking long.

With renewed clarity, he knew what he had to do to protect Skylar.

He had to let go.

He had to let go, and let the wolf take control.

The first two floors were all humans, high on meth. None had put up much of a fight when they had tied them up.

"Let's do this nice and easy. I don't want a big shit show…" Damon's words were cut off by a predatory growl from upstairs.

"Think we found Zane," Jaxon quipped.

"So much for nice and easy." Jayden tightened his hand around the gun. "Bring on the shit show."

IN A BLINDING FLASH, Zane shifted into wolf. Hershel cursed, realizing he no longer had the advantage over him.

One of the guards shot at him, but Zane was too fast, anticipating the bullet and jumping out of the way. He turned and growled at the guard.

Both human guards screamed and popped off another round. Zane dodged the bullets and turned and growled at the humans.

"Fuck this. You don't pay me enough, Wade." The guards

scrambled out of the room, dropping their guns in their escape.

They raced up to the third floor just as the sound of gunfire erupted in the building.

"Fuck," Damon growled as he hit the hallway. "Braxton, call Barrett and tell him the situation is out of control. He's going to have to do some damage control on this one."

Braxton hung back to update their Pack Master as the rest ran toward the room the noise was coming from.

Two terrified humans tore out of the room and raced toward them.

Damon grabbed one and slammed him up against the wall while Lucien grabbed the other one.

"You got to let us go, man. There's a fucking animal in there. He's going to kill us all." The burly man struggled against Damon to get him to let him go, but he only tightened his grip.

"What do you mean?" Damon growled.

"It's a fucking werewolf like in one of those movies. You got to let us go, man," the other guard cried out.

"Fuck." Lucien glanced at Damon. They both punched the guards in the face. Their limp bodies crumpled to the floor.

"I got these two." Braxton grabbed the unconscious guards by their collars and pulled them toward the nearest room. "I'll let Barrett deal with these two idiots."

CHAPTER 68

Zane growled and lunged for Hershel. They were both in wolf form, but Zane's lust for the red wolves' blood was insatiable.

Zane landed on Hershel and pinned him to the ground with his massive paws. Hershel plowed his claw into Zane's chest where they'd cut him and injected the silver.

Pain shot through his chest, and he was momentarily crippled.

Hershel knocked Zane off and landed on top of him, biting him on the shoulder.

Zane's blood pulsed as Hershel locked his teeth into his skin. What Hershel didn't realize was that with every strike of pain inflicted and every visual of Skylar being hurt, his wolf strength grew.

It was time to end this. It was time to end him.

Using his powerful back legs, he kicked Hershel in the stomach. The red wolf went flying across the room, taking a patch of Zane's hide with him.

Flipping to his feet, Zane registered the fact that the

Guardians had arrived and were filling up the doorway, guns drawn and shouting orders.

Ignoring them, Zane jumped through the air and landed on Hershel, giving him the upper hand in the battle. Fear flashed through the wolf's eyes as Zane bared his teeth and growled. He went for the neck, biting down hard on the throat. Cartilage and bone crackled in his mouth as Zane ripped out his enemy's throat.

Lucien's senses were on high alert as he surveyed the scent in the room.

Skylar was curled into a ball, looking on with horror as Zane ripped the throat out of another wolf. Even that wasn't enough to satisfy his bloodlust. He continued to maul the body, ripping out pieces as blood spurted on the walls and floor.

Lucien growled as he recognized the other Were in the room as Dale Wade, Arkansas's number-one drug dealer, who everyone thought was dead. Yet here he stood, in the flesh and clearly not dead. Dale swung his gun around at the group of Guardians as they entered the room.

"Put the fucking gun down." Lucien aimed his gun at Dale.

"Fuck you." Dale grabbed Skylar's arm and tugged her to her feet. He pressed the gun to her temple and snarled. "This is your entire fucking fault, Skylar. If you hadn't started fucking around with that Guardian, then I wouldn't be in this mess. As usual, you're fucking up my life."

"Dale, put the fucking gun down and let the girl go or I'm

going to put a bullet in your head." Damon flanked Lucien, while Jaxon was on the other side of him.

From the corner of his eye, Lucien spotted Jayden edging his way toward Skylar.

"Why the fuck do you even care about her? Do you know what she is? She's a red wolf, and she's your enemy." Dale laughed.

"Our only enemy is you and your rogue wolves, who are constantly breaking the law and hurting people," Lucien hissed.

"I bet you assholes wouldn't be so quick to sacrifice your lives if you knew what Skylar really was."

The room went silent. Even Zane stopped his attack and turned to face Dale.

"I see I got your attention too, Zane." Dale narrowed his beady eyes and tightened his grip on Skylar's neck. Tears streamed down her face as she struggled to breathe.

"Skylar may look like a hot piece of ass for you Guardian boys, but she's used goods. And we know how you only mate worthy females. None of you would risk your lives for used goods. I know that. Why, the first time Hershel took her, she was thirteen years old. She screamed like she was dying, but we all knew she liked it."

"Shut your fucking mouth, Dale," Lucien warned. He cut his eyes at Zane. The Were's breathing increased and his whole body was trembling.

"I even got me a piece after Hershel made her pass out." He bent his head to her cheek and grinned. "You wouldn't remember,

Skylar, but I was actually your first. Not Hershel."

Skylar's eyes widened in terror and her body convulsed as she struggled to get away.

"You're a sick fuck, Dale, and if you think you're walking out of here alive, you are wrong," Damon growled.

"That's exactly what I'm going to do, dumbass, because I got some insurance." His grip on Skylar tightened. "And his name is Zane. That crystal meth he got injected with was our latest serum.

We created it so werewolves couldn't control their shift anymore. Once the human population realizes what walks among them, it's going to start a race war between us and them. We are stronger than fucking humans, and we are going to destroy every one of them until it's just Weres running the earth." Dale's eyes glistened with delight. "It's going to be paradise. And I'm going to lead us all."

"You've been smoking too much of your own product, Dale," Damon growled as he leveled his gun at Dale. "There's no way we're going to let that happen."

Lucien glanced at Jayden, who was a few feet away from Skylar. He just needed to distract Dale a few more seconds.

"You're not leaving this room with Skylar," Lucien said.

Zane growled. Dale took the gun off Skylar for a second and aimed it at Zane, who took a step toward him. It was the opportunity Jayden needed.

Jayden grabbed Skylar and shoved her toward the door. Lucien grabbed her and pulled her safely behind him.

Dale growled, swung his gun toward Jayden, and fired.

Zane leapt through the air just before the gun went off. He landed in front of Jayden, taking the impact of the bullet to his side.

Wide-eyed, Dale realized he no longer had anything to leverage. He glanced at the door and swung his gun from Zane to the other Guardians.

Zane stumbled as the silver coursed through his body. His vision blurred and then turned black as he hit the floor with a thud.

"SKYLAR, tell them not to hurt your daddy, now." Dale kept his eyes and his gun aimed at the Guardians. "You tell them not to hurt me, you hear?"

"Don't hurt him." Skylar heard herself say. She clutched the automatic rifle left by the guards in her hands and stepped out from the shadows. "I want to do it."

Dale's eyes widened for a brief second before she squeezed off a rapid-fire round straight into his chest. She aimed for his head and put a bullet there as well.

Dale Wade's body crumpled to the floor.

Damon slid next to her and grabbed the gun from her hand.

"He's dead now, Skylar. He won't hurt you again."

She nodded once and looked around for Zane.

A Guardian with blond hair was bending over him, pressing his own T-shirt to his wound.

Snapping out of her shock, she ran to Zane and pressed her face to his fury chest. The T-shirt over the wound was saturated in his blood. He struggled to breathe as his eyes rolled back into his head. "Don't you dare die on me!"

CHAPTER 70

Barrett arrived just as the red-haired female put a round of bullets into Dale Wade. He shoved his way into the room and surveyed the bloody scene with trepidation.

"I said no shit show." He glared at Damon. "This reeks of a shit show."

"Couldn't be helped, boss." Damon shrugged and nodded toward Zane. "Did Braxton fill you in on everything?"

"Zane's been infected with a special crystal meth and is out of control, there are humans who have seen him shift, and Dale Wade isn't dead." Barrett glared at the body on the floor. "Well, he wasn't dead."

"Yep. Oh, and Zane has been shot with a silver bullet." Damon turned his back so the Guardians who were working on Zane couldn't see his face. "Even if we get the silver out, there's still the problem of his inability to control his shift. He's still a liability."

Ignoring Damon's concerns, Barrett headed for his hurt Guardian.

Kneeling down, he assessed Zane's chest wound and the bullet wound. There was a third wound where flesh had been torn away from his shoulder. "Zane, I know you can hear me. I know you're in there. So you better fucking listen to your Pack Master." Zane opened his eyes and blinked once.

"I'm going to dig this silver bullet out of your side. It's going to hurt like fuck, but there's no way around it. I've also got to get the silver out of this other wound. It looks like they skinned you and just poured liquid silver in. I've got to take more flesh out, and that's going to hurt too. Once it's out, you can heal the wound on your shoulder."

"Is he going to die?" Skylar looked up at him with earnest eyes.

"Not today."

"Am I going to die?" she asked. "I did kill my father, and the Pack Law says the penalty for killing your parents is death. Am I going to die?"

He pulled his knife out of his back jean pocket and flipped up the blade. He turned to her.

"You can't kill someone who's already dead. And if people found out that Dale wasn't dead to begin with, then that would require a *whole lot* of paperwork. And if there's one thing I hate, it's paperwork." He glared.

"He's right." Jaxon knelt beside Zane, ready to assist Barrett.

"Barrett hates paperwork."

Skylar's shoulders sagged in obvious relief. "Thank you." "Don't thank me until we fix Zane."

CHAPTER 71

Zane woke up in a bed in the Guardians' infirmary. His back ached like a bitch and every muscle in his body was sore.

"He's awake." Skylar's voice had him turning his head.

"How do you feel?" She leaned down and cupped his face.

"Step back and let me have a look-see. Boy, you look like you've been run over and dragged ass-backwards in the streets." Dr. Gilliam, the Pack doctor, stepped up and shone a penlight into his eyes. Dr. Gilliam looked more like a mad scientist with his gray hair poking up in all directions. He'd been the Guardian's personal doctor for years, and despite his crappy bedside manner, he was one of the best.

"Cut that shit out." Zane waved away the old man.

"I need to check your vitals." The crotchety old doctor frowned.

"I'm fine. My body just hurts like hell." He scowled as he tried to sit up.

"You've been out for a week." Skylar grabbed his hand and pressed it to her chest. "I didn't think you were ever going to wake up after Barrett dug the silver out."

He ran his hand across his side where the bullet had gone in. The wound was completely healed. He moved his hand up to his chest where the silver had been poured in. That was healed as well.

"Your shoulder is taking more time to heal than the other places," she said.

He touched his fingertips to the rough patch of skin where Hershel had pulled flesh out with his teeth.

"If nothing else, you can always cover it with ink." Barrett stepped up to his bedside with Lucien, Jaxon, Braxton, and Jayden behind him.

"Thank you." Zane looked around his band of brothers. "But I'm still going to be a problem. I didn't find a cure for what I have been injected with. I'm still a danger to our Pack." His stomach turned as he faced his new reality.

"So is that it? Do you think so little of us?" Lucien sulked.

"You are my brothers, and I'm trying to do the right thing here, if you'd shut the hell up." Zane swallowed the lump in his throat.

"I can't be a Guardian if I can't control my shift."

"Zane, you've not shifted in a week." Skylar smiled.

"I've been out, that's why." He hated this. He hated losing his brothers, his job, Skylar, but he had to do the right thing by them all.

"No, it's not," Dr. Gilliam said. "I ran your bloodwork and compared it to the blood sample we got when you first came in. The drug is out of your system. You were only infected one time. While it did take a while to get out of your system, it didn't change your DNA. You are back to normal." The doctor slapped him on the shoulder. "Well, back to your old self, I should say." He made his exit.

"Is that true?" Zane's heart leapt, and he looked to Barrett for confirmation. His hand squeezed Skylar's. He inhaled deep, and Skylar's scent of strawberries and spice flooded his nose. He could smell her. Finally.

"It's true." Barrett grinned and looked around at his Guardians. "You assholes need to get out of here so Zane can rest and spend time with Skylar."

His head hit the pillow as he sucked in a deep breath. One by one, the Guardians said goodbye. Jayden lingered behind.

"I'll go get you some water. I'll be right back." Skylar pressed a kiss to his lips and gave them some privacy.

Zane spoke. "Hey man, I want to thank you for protecting Skylar." He realized his beef with his sister really had nothing to do with Jayden. Zane had just needed someone else to blame for their failing relationship.

"It's what we do, man. No need to thank me." Jayden shoved his hands in his pockets and frowned. "Zane, I should be thanking you. You took that bullet when it was meant for me. The thought that I wouldn't be here with Haley scared the fuck out of me." "It's what brothers do." Zane nodded.

Jayden grinned and stuck out his hand and they shook.

"You can't go in there, ma'am," Dr. Gilliam shouted as the door swung open.

"I can go wherever I want to." Granny huffed as she, Haley, and Ava barged into the room and right up to Zane's bedside.

Barrett and Skylar came back in to see what the fuss was about.

Zane frowned, and Granny took his hand and pressed her lips together.

"Granny, he's resting and doesn't want you to bore him." Jayden gave Zane an apologetic look.

"I've got something to say and I'm saying it." She glared at him and then at the doctor, who threw up his hand and stomped out of the room.

"Zane Steele, I want to thank you for saving my grandson's life. I don't know what I would do if something had happened to him." Her lips quivered and she blinked her eyes to hold back the tears.

Haley bent down and pressed a kiss to his cheek. "Thank you, Zane."

"You're welcome." He shifted uncomfortably. He wasn't used to all this attention.

"Granny, can you please give Zane some peace now?" Jayden took her arm to escort her away.

He stopped and pointed to the large Band-Aid covering her upper arm.

"What happened to your arm?" He frowned. "Did you fall?"

"No, I didn't fall." She shot him a glare. "And I don't appreciate your suggesting I did."

"Sorry." He held up his hands. "Didn't mean to offend. So what happened?"

Haley giggled and covered her mouth.

"Yeah, Granny, show them what happened." Ava snorted.

"Fine." She tugged at the corners and carefully pulled off the Band-Aid. She smiled brightly as she showed off her arm. "I got some ink."

Jayden's mouth dropped and he turned pale. The women giggled, and Zane could swear he heard Barrett mutter, "Fuck my life."

Zane was confused and then stunned. Granny had a bright pink dick tattooed on her arm.

"That shit better be temporary." Jayden's face turned bright red.

He tried to slap the Band-Aid back on, but it fell right back off. "Ouch." Granny scowled. "It's still tender."

"Holy shit, you mean it's real?" Jayden asked, his voice getting louder.

"Of course it is." Granny lifted her chin. She looked at Barrett and showed her arm. "Do you like my rocket ship?"

"Is that what they're calling it these days?" Barrett closed his eyes and rubbed his temple.

"Granny, that's not a rocket ship," Jayden said. "It's a dick on your arm."

Zane bit his lip to keep from laughing.

"Of course it's a rocket ship. I always had a thing for Buzz Aldrin. He seemed to always have that mysterious twinkle in his eye. Neil Armstrong was pretty hot too." She grinned.

"Oh god, just kill me now," Jayden muttered.

"If Matt did that tattoo, I'm going to kill him." Barrett glared at the old woman.

"He most certainly did not." She narrowed her eyes at him. "He refused to do it when I came in. So I had to find someone else."

"The name. Give me the name." Barrett spoke slowly, but everyone could hear the anger boiling beneath the words. "A guy named Tommy."

"Where's his shop?" Barrett pushed.

"I don't think he has one. He did it out of his parents' basement. He said he needed the money for art school." Granny smiled. "I am always a supporter of the arts and higher education. So I killed two birds with one stone."

"Keep your eyes closed," Zane called out to her over the roar of the Harley.

"My eyes are closed," she said. She tightened her hold on his waist as he sped down the road. The cool air whipped through her loose hair, and the bright sun warmed her face. Riding with Zane always made her feel better about life.

It had been three months since Zane had been shot. Two months since she'd finished Ava's house, and one month since the town of Jonesboro had torn down the abandoned apartments due to drug activity.

She had been in a funk since then.

She'd tried looking around for other buildings, but nothing was in her price range.

Zane slowed his speed until he came to a stop. Killing the engine, he flipped the kickstand and slid off the bike first.

"Keep them closed," he said near her ear as he slid his arms around her waist and picked her up off the bike.

She giggled as he set her on her feet and gently kissed both cheeks.

He swung her up in his arms and began to walk.

"What's going on? You're being very secretive."

"More secretive than when we put that flaming pile of dog shit on Damon's front stoop?"

"Yes." She laughed as she recalled the look on Damon's face when he realized he'd stepped in dog shit trying to put out the fire. He'd assumed Jayden had done it and was determined to prank him back.

She'd never seen Zane so relaxed before, and it was good to see him interacting with his fellow Guardians. Since she'd finished working on Ava's house, he'd invited her to come stay with him in Little Rock until she got her next job.

Truth be told, she was in no rush to find another contracting job. She had a lot of money in the bank after finishing Ava's house. She was still determined to find another building to fix up for her girls' home. She knew it would come along. She just had to be patient.

The smell of autumn was in the air, and from the scent of turning leaves and brown grass, she realized they must be out in the country, away from the city limits of Little Rock.

He set her gently on her feet and covered her eyes with his hand.

"Open them."

She opened her eyes and blinked against the bright sunlight. She smiled in confusion as she saw all the Guardians from Little Rock standing in a line in the middle of a pasture.

"What's going on?" She looked up at Zane.

Barrett stepped forward.

"Zane told me about the project you had in mind in Jonesboro." He cocked his head.

"He did?" She blushed. Would the Pack Master think it a stupid idea?

"And when they condemned and tore the apartments down, it got me to thinking." He propped his hands on his hips. "It would probably be a better idea to build your safe haven for girls in a centrally located place in the state. Like Little Rock."

She nodded. "I've been looking around in town, but everything is so expensive."

"Maybe you should look out of town and start from the ground up. Like here." He waved his hand over the pasture.

"That's going to be well out of my budget. The cost to build it would be astronomical."

"Not if money is no object." Barrett motioned toward the people standing in front of them. They parted, revealing a sign that read *Future home for girls — SKYLAR'S HOUSE.*

She shook head. "I don't understand."

"This is your land, Skylar. It's bought and paid for. There's even an account set up in your name with six million dollars in it to build it however you want," Zane whispered in her ear.

"But who bought it?" She looked up at him, her eyes filling with tears.

"We did." Victoria and Richard Steele stepped forward from the crowd of Guardians. Victoria's hair was pulled into a loose bun, and she was dressed in skinny black pants and crisp white top and ballet flats, looking like she'd stepped off the pages of a magazine. Richard looked a bit more relaxed in his khaki pants and golf shirt. She'd never seen him wear anything other than suits.

"Hey, honey." Victoria pulled her into a hug. "We've missed you so much."

"Hey, Skylar. I'm glad to see you." Richard hugged her next.

She wiped the tears from her face as Zane pulled her into his embrace.

"You did this? For me?" She looked up into his parents' faces.

"Zane told us about what happened and how disappointed you were. We got in contact with Barrett, and he helped find us land that was available and set up the deal. We bought the land, but Barrett funded the building account himself," Victoria whispered. "Don't go around telling everyone. The last thing I need is for everyone to start asking for a dollar." Barrett scowled and hurried away.

"I don't know what to say." She looked at Zane's parents. "Thank you. I will never be able to repay you for this."

"Actually, there is a way you can repay us." Richard gave her a wink. "Zane has something he wants to ask you."

She turned to face Zane. His smile had vanished, and he stared at her intensely.

"Skylar, I have never met anyone who is as caring and loving and giving as you are. When I am with you, all I can think about is how lucky I am, and when I'm away from you, all I can think about is seeing you again." He swallowed. "I don't want another day to go by without knowing that you are mine."

"What?" Her heart jumped in her chest. Love swelled up inside her.

"Skylar, I love you more than anything else in this world. I want to be with you for the rest of my life. I want to have children and raise a family with you. Skylar, will you be my mate?"

"I love you, Zane. You know that. But…" She looked at his parents and her heart broke. "You deserve to be with someone that your family will be proud of."

"Skylar Wade, I want you to know that you have always been so precious to us." Victoria blinked back her own emotional tears. "I know that you've had a difficult life, but I also know that whatever has happened has never affected our opinion of you. We love you unconditionally, and we would be proud to have you in our family."

"So you would, in fact, be doing us a very large favor if you agreed to be Zane's mate." Richard grinned.

Tears flowed down her cheeks as she buried her face in Zane's chest. He held her tight and let her cry. After a minute, he pulled back and looked a bit worried.

"Skylar, you didn't answer my question. Don't leave me hanging here." Zane frowned.

"I love you, Zane. I always have." She laughed. "I would love to be your mate. Forever."

His mouth descended on hers in a hot kiss. She held onto him as her chest filled with more love than she'd ever known.

The End

ABOUT THE AUTHOR

Jodi was born and raised in Mississippi. Her deep Southern roots and love of the paranormal led her to write Southern Paranormal novels. She currently lives in Northeast Arkansas with her handsome husband, brilliant son, a temperamental swan, and yellow lab that is fond of retrieving turtles when duck season is over.

Find her on Facebook: **Jodi Vaughn, author**
Follow her on Twitter: **@JodiVaughn1**
Sign up for her newsletter and check out her website:
http://jodivaughn.com
Find her on Instagram: **VaughnJodi**

ALSO BY JODI VAUGHN

Werewolf Guardian Romance Series
Her Werewolf Bodyguard (book 1)
Her Werewolf Protector (book 2)
Her Werewolf Defender (book 3)
Her Werewolf Champion (book 4)

The Vampire Housewife Series
Lipstick and Lies and Deadly Goodbyes (book 1)
Merlot and Divorce and Deadly Remorse (book 2)
Bullets and Booze and Dead Suede Shoes (book 3)
Aces and Eights and Dead Werewolf Dates (book 4)
Veiled Series
Veiled Secrets (book 1)
Veiled Enchantment (book 2)

Somewhere Texas Series
Saddle Up (book 1)
Trouble in Texas (book 2)
Bad Medicine (book 3)
Somewhere in Paradise (book 4)

Cloverton Series

www.ingramcontent.com/pod-product-compliance
Lightning Source LLC
Chambersburg PA
CBHW050403260626
47156CB00003B/850